METATRON

The Mystical Blade

Laurence St. John

METATRON: THE MYSTICAL BLADE

http://www.laurencestjohn.com

SECOND EDITION Paperback

Ogopogo Books - www.OgopogoBooks.com

May 15, 2017

ISBN: 978-1-77223-293-6

Cover design by Ryan Doan: www.RyanDoan.com

Praise for Metatron: The Mystical Blade

"St. John has done it again with *The Mystical Blade*; another novel 13 year olds of any age will really enjoy!" —Piers Anthony, *New York Times* bestselling fantasy author of the *Xanth* series

"St. John's stories are full of warm characters that shine like the sun and deliver the sense of urgency and leadership that is lacking in our youth today. *The Mystical Blade*—a very necessary piece of literary fiction missing in our society." —Braxton A. Cosby, award-winning author of *Protostar*

To my inspiring sister-in-law Mary Lou Davis who rose above her fears and balled her fists as she fought the battle valiantly. In the end, she lost the fight September 2013, defeated by her nemesis—Ovarian Cancer.
You are missed dearly.

Acknowledgements

Above all, I am thankful and grateful to God. For without him, there would be no story.

Special thanks to my editor and trusted friend, Paula Berinstein, for working with me on this second novel.

To *New York Times* bestselling author Piers Anthony who has always answered my questions; I appreciate you very much.

To Mr. Bryce Davis and Storm who helped me visualize the book cover.

I want to express my sincere gratitude to Cheryl Tardif and the team at Imajin Books for their on-going support and enthusiasm for my books.

To my awesome wife, Julie, my most critical reader and editor.

And finally, to my grandchildren Kendall, Eli, Sadie, Evelyn and Harper for being my inspirations.

Chapter 1

If Tyler Thompson had known how tough it was to be a superhero, he might never have gotten involved in the first place. Sure, it was cool having *Flash* speed and super vision and all that, but there was a lot of pressure, and you couldn't *tell* anyone. Not to mention that every time he went out he took his life in his hands and the whole thing was exhausting. Who knew that superheroes got tired? He wasn't sure if being a superhero was a gift or a curse.

So when he heard a cry on the way home from another night of whupping Las Vegas bad guys, he wasn't exactly in the mood for more trouble. In fact, he was tempted to ignore it. But superheroes never ignore people in trouble, no matter what. And while he wasn't one hundred percent superhero yet, he'd never get there if he didn't do his duty.

There it was again—a piercing, high-pitched cry from above, this time followed by the distinct sound of two loud gunshots reverberating off the high-rise buildings. A split second after that, there came the horrific wail of someone in severe pain. Tyler wondered if such noises really could wake the dead, and an image of his dad flickered through his mind. At least his dad's murderer, Dr. Mason Payne, the evil scientist who had tried to kill him too, was safely in jail.

But there was no time for musing. From Hacienda Avenue Tyler looked up at the multi-story Mandalay Bay parking garage and spotted someone bending backwards over a concrete wall. The person's arms were hanging downward, creating the impression that they were preparing to dive backwards. Then a pair of glasses and a set of keys dropped and landed in the flower bed at the base of the structure.

In a flash Tyler was at the top floor of the garage. With his heart racing, he hid behind a cold and damp concrete partition, then peeked out. About ninety feet away he caught a glimpse of a parked silver-colored

BMW 760 with the driver's side door open. Two tall, stocky men were standing behind it. Tyler ducked back behind the partition, threw back his black hood and removed his ski mask so he could wipe away an eyelash. Another thing they didn't tell you about being a superhero. Tyler muttered under his breath, pulled his mask back over his face and flung the hood over his head just as a rush of adrenaline flooded his body.

He'd pay for this later, but it didn't matter because everyone was counting on him. He'd made a promise to his dad, and he wasn't about to let him down. His mom, brother and sister would be expecting big things from him, and Kendall, Master Tanaka and his friend Gabriel were all watching him. Most of all, there was God, who'd given him these powers for a reason and who was surely expecting a lot from a thirteen-year-old boy, even one who had *Flash* speed, an impenetrable force field and an extraordinarily high intellect. But he couldn't think about all that now. The world was in trouble, and he had to fix it.

He looked again, and now the men were carrying pry bars. With his enhanced vision, he could also see handguns stuck in the waistbands in the back of their pants. From out of the shadows, he began creeping towards them just as one of them happened to see him out of the corner of his eye. The man backhanded the other, whispering loudly, then pointed and said, "Hey, boss, take a look. We got company."

Tyler crossed his arms and took a defiant stance. The man roared with laughter. "What's this, a vigilante?"

The other guy smirked. "You mean a wannabe superhero."

Tyler stood his ground.

"Hey, buddy," the boss hollered in Tyler's direction. "Superheroes don't exist. They're only in comic books and movies." Both guys practically busted a gut laughing and giving each other high-fives.

Unfazed, Tyler yelled, "Drop the guns and put your hands up." What a cliché. Sometimes he sounded so silly to himself.

"Hey, he sounds like a kid," the non-boss said. The men began laughing again, this time almost crying.

"Shoot him," the boss ordered.

There was silence. "But he's only—"

Angry now, the boss practically barked. "Do it before he gets any closer and can identify us."

Immediately the other guy pulled his gun from his waistband and fired two rounds at Tyler. Like magic, Tyler evaded the bullets, which were ricocheting off pillars and flying all over the place, without losing a stride as he kept approaching the men. "Is that all you got?" he yelled back.

"What the—" one of the men mouthed. He aimed at Tyler again, then squeezed off four more rounds, but Tyler evaded the bullets with ease. He ran using his *Flash* speed, then, standing almost face to face with the bad guy, performed a high-impact inside forearm block, which released the man's grip on the gun just as he was firing another round.

This time, the bullet missed Tyler's ear by a hair. The gun flew up towards the ceiling, then slid across the parking garage floor. The man began throwing a flurry of punches, but Tyler easily deflected them. Still, he must have known some martial arts because the next thing he did was throw various kicks. But Tyler had had enough and gave the man a penetrating front kick to his sternum, then a smashing roundhouse kick to his temple, knocking him out.

By that time, the boss had sprung open

the trunk of the BMW to reveal two large metal cases with "FR23" written on them. As Tyler approached, the boss glanced down at his pry bar, then swung it at his head three times, as if he were swatting at flies, just missing him by fractions of an inch on each attempt.

"Hey! You little punk!" he yelled as Tyler executed an outside block while sliding first his hands, then his arms around the big man like a snake, locking his arms to his body. Acting like a human boa constrictor, Tyler applied pressure until the man dropped the pry bar, which clanked while bouncing off the floor. Tyler quickly placed the man in a wrist lock and guided him to a kneeling position. The man grunted, then screamed in pain. Tyler performed a knife strike to his neck, rendering him helpless. Then he reached under his black hoodie and pulled out a set of nylon flex handcuffs. He threw both men in the backseat of the BMW and cuffed them together.

From behind him, Tyler heard moaning. He turned around and saw a man leaning against the concrete wall bleeding from both legs. "Hold on, I'm calling for help," Tyler yelled in his not-yet-deepened voice as he placed a call to 911. Then, as fast as a cheetah, he pulled off his hoodie, tore it into strips and tried to stanch the bleeding.

When he heard the sirens, he took off like the flick of a switch. It wouldn't do to be discovered. Chalk up another one for the good guys. All was well with the world. Well, at least in Las Vegas. He was living the dream, as he'd hoped he would when he discovered that he had Metatron's superpowers. But if everything was going so well, why wasn't he happier? Oh, that's right. He wasn't a full-fledged superhero yet, and it was driving him crazy not knowing whether he ever would be.

Tyler sat on a bench in front of the Flamingo Hotel, removed his ski mask and shoved it into his back pocket. Of course he was happy. Why shouldn't he be? How many other people got to do cool things like run faster than the wind and shrink themselves to the size of a cricket whenever they wanted to? Maybe he was feeling some kind of chemical letdown. He'd read about things like that. Oh well. If that was all it was, it'd be over soon. No sense sitting here and wallowing.

Brightening, he went to retrieve his

hidden backpack where he had stowed it—in the usual spot on top of the overhang covering the entrance to his favorite Italian restaurant, Battista's Hole in the Wall. Munching on a Snickers bar, he headed home, bouncing like a rap star and acting like he owned the city. He was tempted to yell from the rooftops, but he knew better. When all was said and done, this was between him and Metatron, the angel who had bequeathed his special powers to the One, that special person who would save the world. He was pretty sure Metatron would not like it if his identity became known—if he truly were the One. This wasn't about glory. It was serious business.

He desperately wanted to know if he was. This being up in the air was agony. He wanted to be able to put out huge forest fires or halt devastating tsunamis or even stop wars. Imagine making *that* kind of a difference. Of course, if not, he could still save innocent people from bad guys. Nothing wrong with that. But sometimes he just felt that there was so much to do that even his best efforts were too puny.

As he was thinking that dreary thought, his Seether alarm ringtone sounded. He pulled out his cell phone. "Oh no. School starts in fifteen minutes. I gotta go!"

He was almost late for his first class. He was participating in a special program that let gifted middle and high school students spend half days taking classes at the University of Las Vegas. As if trying to keep up with college students at thirteen weren't difficult enough, Tyler had chosen physics and chemistry, which were about as challenging as you could get. He couldn't afford to be distracted, and now his nighttime activities were catching up with him.

He struggled to keep his eyelids open, but sleep was inevitable. He was so warm and comfortable and—*smack*! Dr. Bodi slammed his teacher's edition of *Advanced Physics* on the top of Tyler's desk, nearly causing him to pee his pants.

"Mr. Thompson, now that you're awake and I have your undivided attention, you've been summoned to Dean Anderson's office. Someone is here to see you."

"Uh oh," Tyler mumbled. "Not again."

"Tyler," Dean Anderson said calmly as he leaned forward in his posh leather chair and breathed his repulsive coffee and cigarette breath into Tyler's face, "this is the fifth time you have been in my office for sleeping and snoring in class." The dean paused and looked at Mr. Weaver, Tyler's middle school athletic director, who had been summoned to the conference. "What do you have to say? Having your parents come in for conferences didn't seem to help. Talking with one of our finest counselors hasn't helped. So are you going to come clean with me this time? Are you doing drugs?"

Tyler grimaced, then leaned back to get away from that awful-smelling breath. "No, Mr. Anderson, I don't do drugs," Tyler said gripping the arms of his chair. "I'm, er, busy. I go to college half a day, then to my own school the other half. I have karate class three times a week. I also teach two karate classes, I'm on the school's football team, I have a girlfriend and I have a night job! Anyway, I've read the UNLV's policies and I don't recall anything about students getting in trouble for sleeping in class."

"Not if you're a regular student. But you are here representing Logan Prep. You are setting a bad example. I'm sure you don't want to jeopardize the opportunity for other Logan students to take advantage of this great program."

Tyler thought of Kendall and Lukas. They had a good chance of making it in themselves in a couple of years. He certainly didn't want to mess things up for them.

"Also, this is this first I've heard of you having a night job. Doing what, might I ask?"

"I-I volunteer at the Las Vegas Police Department," Tyler replied. *I'm not telling them what I really do.*

"Well, Tyler, you may be very smart and one of Logan Prep's best wide receivers, but we have rules," said Dean Anderson. He almost looked depressed. "This pains me to say, but Mr. Weaver has informed me that your principal is placing you on probation and banning you from playing any sports until you can get this problem under control."

Tyler threw his head back in disgust, mouth slightly opened. "Aw, man, that's not fair. For how long?"

"We'll just have to wait and see. It all depends on you." He waited a beat. "You don't have to be a superhero, you know."

Tyler started. How did he know? Then he realized that the dean was speaking metaphorically.

"And by the way, Tyler, you have detention tonight after school," Mr. Weaver said, adding insult to injury.

As Tyler left the dean's office, he was still feeling stung, but he was pretty sure he'd better change his ways. If he didn't straighten up, they might cancel the program! Not only that, but his coach and teammates were counting on him to help achieve their first undefeated season. How was he going to manage crime-fighting, school, sports, a girlfriend? A superhero should be able to figure this out. He'd have to think harder.

After school and detention, Tyler raced to his taekwondo class. He didn't want to use his powers all the time. He couldn't stay in shape that way, and anyway, what if he forgot and gave himself away?

He was now quite late and his girlfriend, Kendall, was upset, so he gave her a mile head start. Usually they ran side by side and caught up on the day's events. Since he was more advanced then she was, he would also coach her and keep her motivated. But now it was a mad dash.

Despite Kendall's head start, Tyler was immediately five feet in front of her. She took a deep breath. "Hey, you scared the heck out of me! Stop using your powers."

Of course he had told *her* about them. After all, Kendall was his girlfriend. But sometimes she didn't like it if he used his abilities when he didn't have to.

"Come on, keep going. We're almost there," Tyler shouted back with a grin on his face, but his smile faded when he glanced up at the street lights. There, at the top of every one, was a big old honkin' white and brown ferruginous hawk just staring at him. They gave him the creeps. He glanced over at Kendall, but she had passed him and was a hundred yards ahead.

Of course he had to wait for her in the end. While he was biding his time in front of Pat Tanaka's taekwondo school, Tyler felt that Jedi intuition that somebody was watching him. He looked around and spotted a huge black Bentley with its windows blacked out pulling into the rundown strip mall parking lot. He followed it intently with his eyes as it stopped a few rows back from the school. The only image he could make out inside the vehicle was what looked like a pair of red, glowing eyes. This he couldn't resist. He just had to get closer. But as soon as he'd taken a few steps towards the vehicle, Kendall arrived. He couldn't involve her in whatever this was. It could be dangerous. The Bentley would have to remain a mystery.

"'Bout time, slow poke," Tyler chuckled chuckle as he ran towards her.

"Very funny," she replied, then stuck her tongue out at him.

He slid his finger across the face of his cell phone. "Not bad. Three miles in thirty minutes. I think you're almost ready for your test."

"Thanks," she replied, bending down to tie her shoelace. "Wait up!"

As Tyler reached for the door handle, his phone dinged, indicating that he had received a text. He stopped dead in his tracks. "Now what does Mom want?" he muttered. As he read the message, his face fell. It wasn't from his mom. It had come from an unknown cell number. It read, *your family will pay along with your precious girlfriend. I'm one step closer. And remember, I always have a backup plan.*

Staring down at the sidewalk, Tyler let out a long sigh, then closed his eyes. Superhero, school, karate, Kendall, red crazy eyes, and now this. He really would have to be a superhero to handle it all.

Chapter 2

Kendall body-slammed right into Tyler's back. She hadn't been paying attention to where she was going, but he wasn't bothered. He was used to her zoning out. Kendall was so curious about the world that she'd lose track of what she was doing and start thinking about something else. It was one of the things he especially liked about her.

He turned his head to the left, then to the right, scanning the entire parking lot. The black Bentley was gone.

"What's wrong?" Kendall said.

Tyler was silent for a few seconds, then replied, "Oh nothing. Just a message from UNLV."

It wouldn't do to worry her by telling her what he had just read. Still, *he* was a bit freaked out. He didn't like the idea of anyone threatening his family, even as a joke. Not after everything that had happened.

"Come on," he said as he entered the school. The lovebirds gave each other a quick hug and went to their respective locker rooms to change into their uniforms.

Soon Tyler was standing in front of the class sporting his black belt with a newly stitched third gold stripe. He had passed his third degree black belt test with ease a few months ago and his second degree almost six months ago. For a thirteen-year-old that was a tremendous accomplishment. Sometimes he worried, though. Even though the powers enhanced his natural abilities, he never used them in class. He could never be sure that they hadn't changed him in ways he wasn't aware of. What if he were cheating without knowing it? Especially while he was teaching and all eyes were on him, as they were today.

Tyler pushed the thought away. "Okay, practice what you have learned today at home. Now go get your sparring gear!" he called out.

As he opened his mouth to bark the next instruction, he felt the same familiar presence he had earlier in the parking lot. But this time it was more pronounced. He peered out the window and saw a tall figure dressed in a black hooded cloak-like outfit, something like the Grim Reaper but without the scythe, standing in the parking lot looking at the karate school. The figure neither moved nor spoke, but when Tyler blinked, it was gone.

He closed his eyes and breathed slowly the way Master Tanaka had taught him, and searched his feelings while the class full of black belts and less adept students scrambled to strap on their equipment. Random images and thoughts were running wild in his mind. He was trying to figure out if that thing he had seen was real or whether he was just daydreaming. Furthermore, how could a text message be sent from a person in jail? For he had a strange feeling that none other than Mason Payne had sent it, and he was definitely in jail.

Payne had been the lead scientist at Steele Corp. until he was caught formulating a drug that could have corrupted children's minds all over the world. He had also been the FBI's prime suspect in the six-year investigation of the murder of Dr. Trevor

Thompson, Tyler's father. He had eventually admitted that he'd killed Dr. Thompson in cold blood. Now he had completed six months of a life sentence. He was a dangerous and devious man, but he was in a maximum security prison. There was nothing to worry about if the message had actually come from Payne, was there?

Moments later Tyler opened his eyes to see all the students standing at attention, waiting for his next command. Master Tanaka was standing beside him, staring at him in the most peculiar way.

"Everything all right, Tyler?" he whispered. "I think you were snoring."

"Yes sir, sorry sir," Tyler replied in a low voice. "I need to talk with you after class."

"Indeed," Master Tanaka replied.

Tyler selected the three highest-ranking black belts to spar with. There was a fourth degree, Joe St. John, and two third degrees, Mr. Razer Jaxsen and Mr. Andy Welling. The others students sat at the back of the dojo to observe. Tyler quickly secured his own foot and hand gear, then offered an explanation.

"When fighting multiple opponents, stay focused, use your instincts and believe in your abilities. Rise above." This was what

Master Tanaka had taught him, and he kept the thought close.

Tyler and the other three black belts bowed to each other. "These are the rules, gentlemen. One, if you are hit twice you're out. Two, if you're knocked down you're out. Three, if you make uncontrolled contact to the face you're out. Any questions?"

"No sir," Razer Joe and Andy said in unison as they surrounded Tyler and formed a triangle shape.

Tyler looked at Master Tanaka, who winked in a way that said, *Take it easy on your opponents.*

Within a split second, Tyler had jumped nearly five feet in the air and performed a powerful scissor kick that struck Joe and Andy directly in their chests and knocked them on their behinds. Razer saw an opening and punched Tyler once in his stomach, taking him totally by surprise. Stunned, Tyler retaliated by performing a sweep kick, which knocked him to the floor, then heel kicked Razer's chest. The fighting went on for a few more minutes with Tyler getting the better of his opponents. After the sparring had concluded, all four guys shook hands. Tyler lined the students back up, then ended the class by saying, "Each one of you is special. Each one of you has the ability to succeed. Believe in yourself and good things will happen. Dismissed." Then he bowed to the class.

In the stinky sweat-filled locker room, Tyler striped off his yucky black and white uniform and stuffed it into his gym bag. The chain and medallion that Master Tanaka had given him hung around his neck. Not only had his techniques and abilities developed and matured, but his body had gone through some transformations. He now had a washboard stomach and his body fat count was only two percent.

As he pulled his shirt on over his head he heard a ding. Forgetting about the earlier text, he smiled as he reached down and removed his cell phone from the side pocket on his gym bag, anticipating that Kendall had left him a mushy text message.

"D3, open," he said. The top half of the cell phone automatically slid open, spun 180 degrees, then flipped up looking something like a satellite dish. He had personally reprogrammed and modified his old DROID phone into his hologram projection phone, which he had named D3. The text read, *Thanks for helping me today. I really appreciate it! At least you finally found time to spend with me. Kendall.* He sat down for a few minutes feeling exhilarated and inadequate at the same time.

As he stared aimlessly at the inside of his locker, he remembered the Bentley, and *that* caused him to remember the mysterious text and the weird birds. It sure was turning into a strange day. Maybe he should go talk to Pat.

After changing into his street clothes, he made his way to Master Tanaka's office. Pat was sitting behind his desk, looking at an old book. When Tyler entered, he looked up and smiled that half-smile he got at the oddest times.

But as he listened, his face became a cipher. He was always like that. Sometimes it drove Tyler nuts. This time, however, he didn't notice. He was too busy telling Pat everything about his strange day.

Master Tanaka told him to search his feelings and he would figure out the meaning behind the message. Tyler crossed to the window, linked his hands behind his back and stood motionless, peering out the window. He began brainstorming, pondering over the remarkable things that had happened to him in the last few months: his visit to AREA 51, his missing grandpa, his angel friend Gabriel, and of course Payne. He scrunched up his face and tried to figure out who the text message was from.

"I'm pretty sure I know who the message is from but I don't think it's possible," he said. "And I'm still unclear what it means by 'closer to it.' Closer to what? And what backup plan? What do you think he's up to?"

"Tyler, if you're referring to Dr. Payne I suspect he is up to no good. People like him don't change. Perhaps it means closer to you, or closer to a new plan or maybe closer to being free? Remember, Payne had or still does have special abilities. But nothing compared to yours."

Tyler turned to Master Tanaka. "But what if he does escape? He said my family and Kendall would pay!"

"Be patient, rise above," Master Tanaka replied.

Tyler rolled his eyes. "I had a feeling you'd say that."

Master Tanaka stood up, walked over to Tyler and placed one hand on his shoulder. "Even if he escaped it would be foolish of him to come after Kendall or your family.

Those are the first places the authorities would be watching."

Tyler felt a little more at ease. "I guess you're right. Thank you, sir."

When Tyler exited the office, he noticed Graeson Payne, Dr. Payne's son, lurking around the corner. Graeson had a huge grin on his face. Tyler glared back but kept walking. When he saw Kendall, he asked, "You ready? My mom is here."

"Yep," Kendall replied with a smile on her face. "It sure is different since your old babysitter Rebekka moved away to college. I was getting used to her picking us up."

Tyler giggled. "You're funny. You know what a pain she was. Remember when she crushed my game on purpose?"

"Yeah, I forgot about that," Kendall said. "What did she have against you anyway?"

"I dunno," said Tyler. "I'm a nice guy. What's not to like?"

As they hopped into the back seat of Tyler's mom's black Chevy Tahoe, he glanced at his mother and mumbled to Kendall. "I think you're ready for your test." Speaking louder, he said, "Oh, Mom, by the way, I'm banned from playing any sports until I get my sleeping issue under control."

Julia glanced at the rearview mirror. "Oh honey. Maybe you should quit or at least cut back on the hours you're putting into your night job."

Julia thought Tyler was working—well, volunteering, since he wasn't old enough to work, for the Las Vegas Police Department. Since Tyler had a deep knowledge of computers, he told her he was the assistant to their information systems employee. Once in a while he would ride along with a police officer, though. Tyler thought this explanation sounded believable. Julia worried about him being out at night, especially since most of the time he had to walk to one or more of the seven police substations, but she was willing to go along with his wishes because she knew he could take care of himself, being a third degree black belt and having special abilities. Plus, she trusted him. If she'd known the truth, well, he worried about that. He wasn't sure how she'd react.

Julia was acting fidgety and seemed to be biting the inside of her cheeks. "Everything okay, Mom? You're acting a little weird." They were approaching the local Burger King, and Julia quickly turned in. "I guess you're not cooking tonight,"

Tyler said and laughed out loud. He took a deep breath. "Mmmmm, I can smell the flame-broiled aroma now."

Julia unlatched her seatbelt and turned to face Tyler. Tears were running down her face. Tyler was taken aback.

"What's wrong, Mom?"

Julia tapped the screen on her iPhone and a breaking news article displayed. "You need to read this, honey."

"What does it say, Tyler?" Kendall asked.

Tyler began reading out loud. "Several hours ago, Dr. Mason Payne escaped from the county jail. His whereabouts are unknown." *I was right!* Shocked, Tyler dropped the phone on the center console and it bounced to the floor. A flurry of emotions raced through his body.

"You're right, Mom. I'm cutting my hours back on my night job. Well, just for a little while. I now have a new mission. A killer needs to be found and put back in jail where he belongs! But there's something I need to do first."

Chapter 3

Throughout lunch, if you consider eating peanut butter out of the container with a spoon lunch, which Tyler was almost sure Julia didn't know he was doing, Tyler could only think of the breaking news article. How Payne had managed to escape was still a mystery. They had mounted a manhunt, but there were no details about any findings. Where could he be now? There was no way Payne would return to the scene of his crime, was there? Graeson was here, of course, but the authorities would be watching him, and Payne would know that, so he wouldn't chance coming to see him. But if Payne couldn't come here, how could he get back at Tyler?

After his brief lunch, Tyler ran upstairs to his room, but not before letting his dog,

Maxx, lick the remaining peanut butter off the spoon before he placed it in the dishwasher. Poor Maxx. He had been through so much. He had been poisoned with Payne's contaminated Dewrilium, which his henchmen, Eli and Devon from Steele Corp., had dumped in a nearby cesspool. That had made Maxx sick. He had broken his front leg after being struck by a passing motorcycle he was chasing. And to top it off, he had been electrocuted when Jude, Tyler's older brother, connected him to a battery charger just to see what would happen. Of course, peanut butter was good for him, so there were no worries there.

Now Maxx was tagging along, still licking the peanut butter from the roof of his mouth. As soon as Tyler entered his room, he heard a voice. It was Gabriel. Gabriel was Tyler's mentor and friend. He was the one who had given him the black case that concealed the iridescent fragment containing the powers of Metatron, which his grandfather had smuggled out of AREA 51. Tyler had his suspicions that Gabriel had superpowers himself, or was an angel. He hadn't seen him since the arrest of Dr. Payne.

"Tyler, you have been most patient about waiting to obtain the remainder of your powers, but now it is time to retrieve them," Gabriel said. "Something unexpected has happened and you must move quickly. Remember what your grandfather's message said."

It had been his grandfather's message that had led him to believe the remaining powers were hidden somewhere in AREA 51. Before it had self-destructed, it had told him that, during the moon landing in 1969, the astronauts had brought back a glowing sphere. The object was rushed to AREA 51, where it would remain dormant until "the One" had been born and marked by God with a unique symbol on his body. When the One retrieved it, it would activate, giving him Metatron's superpowers so he could save Earth from the coming plagues and battles. The message had said nothing about what might happen if someone other than the One took the object, or who the One really was.

Tyler waited for about a minute for more information, but Gabriel was gone. He knew what he had to do. He sat at his computer tapping the keys, browsing the Internet on AREA 51 and its surroundings, trying to figure out how, when and where was the best place to sneak inside. Maxx was sitting on the floor beside him panting the unpleasant scent of peanut butter and dog breath onto his leg.

"There has to be some way to get in there," Tyler mumbled. "I have to get to Metatron's—*my* powers—before Payne. If the powers are in there as Grandpa said they were, Payne must have found them as well, but how?" He was getting frustrated since all his research was leading him to dead ends. Maybe Lukas could help.

Lukas was Tyler's best friend besides Kendall. When Tyler had discovered Payne's Dewrilium plot, Lukas had helped bring him down. That was when Tyler had discovered that Lukas had superpowers of his own. He could literally read the writing on the wall. When Lukas was in second grade, he was taking a test one day and was getting upset because he didn't know some of the answers. He looked up, and there they were on the chalkboard. He thought that it was stupid for the teacher to have written the answers on the board. After class he was talking with some of his friends about what he had seen, and they gave him strange looks. They all told him the chalkboard was blank. He was beginning to feel self-conscious, so he told them he was joking and they had all laughed.

When Tyler heard this story, he was relieved. Knowing that he wasn't the only "freak" had helped him keep the panic at bay, when it struck in the wee hours of the night. Funnily enough, they hadn't talked much about their powers since then. They'd just used them, as if having super senses and abilities were perfectly normal. But now Tyler was wondering if Lukas had the same feelings he did.

Tyler called Lukas then went downstairs to the family room to play video games while he waited. Once Lukas arrived, the boys sat on the edge of the couch wearing their sunglasses on the top of their heads, playing *Rock Band* with Tyler on the guitar and Lukas on the drums. After they finished the third song, Tyler asked for Lukas's help. He told him what he needed to obtain and how he'd have to sneak into AREA 51 and see if he could find his grandfather. Then, before Lukas could answer, Tyler said, "Hey man, how do you deal with your own powers? Do you ever feel like they are overwhelming?"

Lukas glanced at Tyler and rolled his eyes. "Tyler, you have to realize that my ability doesn't even come close to yours. You're a superhero. I'm just someone that can read words on a wall that nobody else can. If I don't want to read it, I just ignore it."

"Your ability did save my life though. And, I'm not a superhero—yet."

"Why do you ask?"

"Well, lately I've been thinking that all this superhero stuff is so challenging. There is always some type of crime happening in the world. I have to lie to my mom and other people about what I do at night. I have regular school plus college courses. I'm involved in taekwondo. I have chores and I have a girlfriend."

"Yes, Kendall can be pretty demanding," Lukas replied chuckling.

"Shut up. I'm being serious!"

"Sorry."

"What I'm trying to say is that this crime-fighting stuff feels so surreal, like maybe it's too much to handle."

"What!" Lukas said dropping his drumsticks. "Tyler, everything you've been through over the past year is enough to send anybody over the edge. But you're only thirteen years old and you're handling it darn well. Sometimes I don't know how you do it all. There's no manual for what you're doing. I'm proud of you, buddy."

"You are?" Tyler replied feeling slightly better about himself.

"Plus the best is yet to come. Once you have all your powers, who knows what you'll achieve."

"Thanks, Lukas. That means a lot to me."

"You're welcome. Are you done whining now so we can get back to playing?" Lukas said raising his eyebrows.

"I wasn't whining, I was venting," Tyler replied as he positioned his guitar for the next song.

Lukas picked up one of his drumsticks positioning it like a light saber. "Tyler, if you have any powers for playing guitar you should use them. You're terrible. And Tyler, you're not a Jedi guitar player, yet," Lukas said trying to speak in an older voice.

"Whatever," Tyler said, laughing. "Speaking of not doing well, you better drink another Monster energy drink. You're missing a lot of notes. Why do you drink that stuff anyway, Lukas? It's not really good for you."

"I mainly buy it for the graphics on the can. It reminds me of you. Look at the green M—Metatron."

"You're so weird, Lukas," Tyler said and smiled while shaking his head.

* * *

After an early dinner that same evening, Tyler talked about AREA 51 with his stepdad, Sean, out on the front porch. Sean was a former FBI informant and analyst at Steele Corp, where Payne had also worked before he was caught. Like Lukas, Sean had been instrumental in foiling Payne's plot and sending him to jail.

"Why do you need to go to AREA 51, Tyler?" Sean asked.

"Since you worked for the FBI you can keep this confidential, right?"

"Of course! What's up?"

Tyler explained to Sean what he and Lukas had talked about. However, he didn't reveal the entire conversation.

"Remember that time when you talked to Gabriel, and Gabriel slipped and said he was secretly helping his friend, Benjamin, with a silver metal that he called Metatron?"

"Yes, I recall something like that, and I believe you said you had never heard of it but it was a cool name."

"I am almost positive the Benjamin that Gabriel was referring to is Mom's dad, my grandpa. I believe he is still alive."

"Are you serious?"

"I wouldn't joke about something like this. But I need to go to AREA 51 to verify that Benjamin is actually my grandfather. Mom will probably freak once she finds out, but she would be so happy. I don't want to say anything to her until I know for sure."

Sean crossed his arms. "Why are you so sure he is there and he is alive?"

"Well," Tyler started as he looked down, then quickly looked back up at Sean. "Gabriel told me. Months ago he gave me a flash drive with a file on it from Benjamin that he said would explain what I was going through. The file said he was my grandfather, among other things, and he was being held against his will at AREA 51."

Sean slowly unfolded his arms. "Okay, Tyler. I trust Gabriel, so I believe what you are telling me is valid." He paused for a moment, lost in thought, then brightened. "Hey, Tyler, you and Lukas are looking at it all wrong. Instead of *breaking* in, maybe you boys can *walk* in."

Tyler looked confused. "I don't understand. AREA 51 is heavily guarded, plus it has three rows of barbed wire fence. How do you walk through that?"

"Well, you know that when I quit informing for the FBI and married your mom, I was appointed the CEO of Steele Corp."

"Right, so how is that going to help?" Tyler interrupted.

"Let me finish," Sean replied. "I received a call today from a scientist at AREA 51 who is interested in the fire retardant experiment we have been testing and getting certifications and patents on. Remember the one you saw at Steele Corp a while back, when the man was sprayed with a flame thrower and he didn't get burnt?"

"Oh yeah, the red spray stuff," Tyler said. "That was cool."

"They want me to demonstrate that same test for them. Let me make a call to the scientist and I'll ask him if it's all right for you and Lukas to go with me to watch the demonstration. Maybe you, Lukas and Maxx can scope out the place and find some clues.

Or even stumble across something. You'll have to be careful, of course. They'll be watching us."

"Wow, that's great!" Tyler gave Sean a quick half hug. "Thanks, Sean. I really appreciate you helping."

Before karate class Tyler asked Master Tanaka for his advice. "Master, I believe the remaining powers are locked up at AREA 51. I was going to try and sneak in somehow, but Sean is going to take me instead. Some scientist wants him to demonstrate an experiment Steele Corp has been testing. But that place is huge so how will I locate them?"

"If you are certain they are there, once inside follow your intuition. You will know when they are close. And Tyler, acquire the remainder of Metatron's—*your* powers—before Payne or anyone else obtains them. If you don't many people could die."

Tyler looked puzzled. "What do you mean people could die? How?"

"That I will explain to you later. However, for now, focus on getting the powers. Gabriel and I will help you. But go at once."

"Does this have to do with what Gabriel

told me? That something unexpected has happened and I must move quickly?"

"Yes it does, but for now your only priority is to obtain the powers."

Chapter 4

Reluctantly, an AREA 51 scientist had agreed to have Tyler, Lukas and Maxx as guests. Sean could be very persuasive when he tried.

The dark blue Steele Corp. company van pulled out in front of Steele Corp. to pick up everyone along with Sean and Kelltie, Sean's lead scientist. Kelltie had been promoted from staff scientist to the company's highest science position almost six months ago. In celebration, she had changed her name from Samantha to Kelltie, confusing absolutely everyone. While standing there, Tyler noticed the writing on the two metal cases.

"Hey, Sean, those cases look kind of scratched up."

"They were actually stolen a while back,

but luckily they were found and not compromised."

"What does FR23 mean?" Tyler asked. Somehow the letter-number combination seemed familiar.

"It stands for Flame Retardant Formula 23," Sean replied.

Then Tyler remembered. These were the cases from the Mandalay Bay parking garage? How in the world did those bad guys get them, and how did they get back here?

Once the two metal cases were inside the van and buckled up, Tyler turned his attention to Kelltie. He couldn't take his eyes off her. She was very attractive for a thirty-something-year-old woman. She had her long blonde hair pulled back in a ponytail. Her slender body made him feel all gooey inside. Almost like the first time he saw Kendall. Lukas and Tyler were sitting behind her, and Tyler reached over the seat.

"Hello, I'm Tyler. Nice to meet you," he said as they shook hands.

"Nice to finally meet you as well, Tyler, since I've only seen pictures of you and your siblings. Sean speaks highly of you."

"He does? Like what?" Tyler said

nervously.

"Well, about how smart you are, how athletic you are and how great you do in karate."

Tyler glanced at Sean. "I didn't know he talked about me at work."

"Sure does. All the time."

Tyler turned beet red. This gorgeous woman talked about him all the time! Or at least heard about him. It was too much for even a superhero to imagine. "You look smart with those black-framed glasses," he stammered.

"You're quite handsome yourself, Tyler," Kelltie replied with a smile on her face.

Suddenly Tyler felt an elbow in his side. "Shut up, Tyler. You shouldn't be saying that stuff. You have a girlfriend," Lukas said.

"What?" Tyler whispered. "I'm just making conversation. Plus she is hot!"

Lukas just shook his head, and the boys were silent for a couple of minutes. Then suddenly a high-pitched squeak came from Lukas's direction. Within seconds a rotten egg smell had filled the air.

Tyler covered his nose. "Lukas!

"My grandfather always told me better

out than in when he farted," Lukas replied
laughing.

But everyone had already rolled down or
cracked their windows.

* * *

Arriving at AREA 51 not a minute too
soon, they went on a planned armed-guard
guided tour. From their nine-passenger
open-top military-style Hummer, Tyler
looked all around for his grandfather and
signs of the remainder of Metatron's
powers. Lukas was looking at all the
building walls and the invisible writing that
was on them.

Tyler tapped the guard on his shoulder
and said that he had read on the Internet that
AREA 51 housed alien spacecraft, aliens
and the actual stage where the moon landing
was shot.

"There's nothing like that here, kid," the
guard sneered. "Don't believe everything
you read."

Tyler then asked a question about a
glowing metal object that had been
recovered from the moon. The scientist in
the front seat looked stunned, then quickly

danced around the question.

"I—I have no idea what you're talking about, young man. Whatever crazy story you heard is nonsense. You kids will believe anything."

"Sorry for asking, sir," Tyler said. "But I have another question." Sean turned around and shook his head from side to side and mouthed the word "no" at Tyler, but Tyler asked anyway. "Have you ever heard of a physicist who works here named Benjamin Steele?"

The guard who was driving swerved, then half turned to Tyler. "That's none of your business, kid. Even if there is a person here by that name, which there isn't, we couldn't disclose that information."

Duly chastened, Tyler sat back and kept looking for signs. There had been total silence for about a minute when Maxx suddenly jumped twenty feet out of the Hummer, then ran around the corner of a huge gray brick and steel building. The driver slammed on his brakes, and Tyler jumped out and ran around the other side of the building to get Maxx.

As he approached the building, Tyler spotted Maxx standing in front of the main door, gazing at it. "What is it, Maxx?" he said tousling the dog's fur. He squatted as he cautiously opened the door just an inch. Maxx began growling. Inside he saw a dozen or so guard dogs being trained. "Not this one, buddy." Tyler looked to his right. "Let's try the next building."

Running side by side, Tyler and Maxx stopped on the north side of the building under the opened window. Tyler heard some humming coming from inside. "This is it, Maxx," he said. He jumped, then pulled himself up like he was doing a pull-up. Looking in through the window, all he saw was a small electric motor that someone was turning on and off.

Disappointed, he let go of the window sill and dropped to the ground. He turned and sat with his back against the building with Maxx next to him. Surveying the area, he sighed. "There's too many buildings. I'll never find it."

Suddenly Maxx stood, tilted his head and pricked up his ears. Then he took off like a bullet. Tyler immediately followed. They were running between two buildings when Maxx stopped abruptly, then barked frantically in front of a large brown building that had no windows and was heavily guarded. Tyler didn't want to cause a scene, so he told him to stop barking.

Suddenly, out of the blue, Tyler got a strange, almost euphoric feeling. He also thought he could hear a faint humming sound. "It's here!" he muttered. He turned his head and went to press his ear against the wall.

Immediately one of the armed security guards hollered at him. "Don't take another step closer. Stop what you're doing and turn around." Tyler froze, but Maxx wouldn't stop barking and began creeping towards the guard, who, despite his superior weaponry, looked threatened. He pulled out a yellow Taser gun and shot Maxx with it. Maxx yelped as he fell over onto the ground. Tyler could see that he was okay, just somewhat paralyzed. Even so, furious thoughts of beating the guard to a pulp raced through Tyler's mind. He took a step towards the guard but immediately stopped when he saw Sean and a dozen armed guards scramble around the corner. Realizing that he'd better keep cool, he calmed himself and gently pulled the prongs from Maxx's side. As he threw the two bloody prongs to one side, he glanced at the guard with an *if looks could kill* look.

He picked Maxx up and cradled him as best he could. "Sean, we're leaving now! If this is how they treat people and animals around here, I don't want any part of this!"

Back in the Hummer, the two scientists were talking in the front seat. One of them turned to Sean. "So, Sean, we really would like to see your experiment. We're most sorry for what happened to your dog. I'll speak to security about this, but perhaps next time you can join us without the dog."

"Well, at least Maxx is okay. Let me check my schedule and I'll see what day I can pencil in," Sean replied.

The two scientists were whispering. Tyler could barely make out what they were saying. One of them glanced back over his shoulder at him.

Sitting next to Tyler, Kelltie patted his leg. "I'm glad Maxx is okay," she said softly. "That really was a mean thing they did to him."

Tyler smiled back. "Thanks. You really are a nice person just like Sean said. Hey, that hurts, Lukas. Cut it out!" he said trying to rub the imprint of Lukas' elbow off his side.

With the tour over and the experiment

postponed, the boys hopped out of the Hummer and ran towards the van.

"Shotgun!" Lukas hollered.

Sean laughed. "Okay, Lukas."

As they pulled up to, then through the heavily fortified guard house, Tyler gasped. His photograph was on the surveillance monitor. The caption below said, *Restricted from unsupervised entry. If seen capture and detain*. Something was up. He'd better be super careful. But why would they be singling him out? Maxx was no threat to them. They'd proved that already.

After they were approximately a quarter mile down the gravel road Tyler turned to Sean. "They were definitely hiding something."

"I believe you're right, Tyler. I believe you're right," Sean replied patting Tyler on the shoulder.

Chapter 5

After the trip to AREA 51, Tyler was certain they were hiding something in that building. He knew he had to get back there before Payne did, so without wasting any time, he devised a plan.

Tyler, Lukas, Kendall and Maxx would take their quad runners and go camping for the weekend up in the Papoose Mountains. Kendall insisted on going to make sure Tyler stayed out of trouble. Of course he didn't tell Kendall or his parents the real reason they were going camping. They were actually going to survey AREA 51.

As they were about to leave, Julia bent down and talked softly to Maxx. "Keep an eye on them and keep them out of trouble."

Tyler smiled. "I heard that, Mom."

"What's that in the trailer next to

Maxx?" Julia asked, pointing at a shiny-looking something.

"Oh, that's my telescope, Mrs. Thompson," Lukas replied. "The mountains are a great place to stargaze."

While Tyler was revving his quad he barely heard his mom saying something. He stopped revving. "What was that mom?"

"I said Sean is riding up tonight. He'll be there sometime before nightfall."

Lukas glanced at Tyler then rolled his eyes.

"Why, mom?" Tyler asked sounding a bit disappointed.

"Kendall's mom called me a little while ago. She said she trusts you of course, however wanted to make sure an adult would be going too. Sean and I thought it would be a good idea as well so Sean volunteered to go."

"Alright, I guess," Tyler said with a heavy sigh.

* * *

After the nearly two-hour trek, Lukas got right to his telescope so as not to waste the remaining daylight. Using his ability to read some data on the sides of a few buildings, he peered through it and read some fresh information about Tyler's grandfather. *We need to relocate Ben right away. The moon meteorite must be better protected. Erect a laser beam field around the meteorite's perimeter. That should keep it secured.*

"What are you looking at, Lukas? I thought this was used for gazing at stars," Kendall said.

"Um, oh, I'm looking at the mountains in the distance. I'm just calibrating it, Kendall. Getting it ready for tonight."

"Can I take a peek?" Kendall asked.

"Sure," Lukas said bumping the telescope over to his left.

Kendall peered into the eye piece. "Wow, the mountains are so close."

"Lukas, can you give me a hand with this?" Tyler called.

Lukas glanced at Tyler. He was unpacking the tent. "Sure, hang on," he said walking over to help Tyler. "I got some stuff to tell you."

"Shh, not now. Later," he said motioning towards Kendall.

* * *

A half hour later, Tyler and Lukas were still struggling to set up the large tent while Kendall and Maxx relaxed and waited under the nearby shade tree.

"Do you guys need any help?" Kendall asked tilting her head sideways. "It looks kind of crooked."

Maxx let out a bark indicating that he agreed. Lukas took a few steps back and laughed. "Well, Tyler, I guess we can't be good at everything."

Kendall got up and walked over to the tent. "This pole goes here and that pole goes there."

"Yes, ma'am," Tyler said pulling his sunglasses down slightly and watching Kendall walk back to the shade tree.

After the poles were switched Tyler clapped his hands once. "Okay, who's hungry?"

"Me, me," Lukas and Kendall sang.

"All right then. I'll get started," Tyler replied beginning to offload the trailer.

* * *

After they had eaten slightly burnt hotdogs, Tyler tossed three large pieces of wood onto the fire and the remainder on the ground about ten feet away. Suddenly he spotted a snake. After taking a second to recover, he stared directly into its eyes and told it to go way while motioning with his hand. The snake raised its body about six inches off the ground, then tilted its head, almost as if it understood what Tyler had said. Seconds later it turned and slithered away.

Sitting by the fire, Lukas and Kendall were still hungry and wanted to make S'mores with Reese's Peanut Butter Cups, so Tyler and Maxx walked over by the quad runners to get the supplies. Tyler turned on the portable CD player, and it began playing Nickelback's song *Gotta Be Somebody* from his mix CD. He walked over and handed the supplies to Lukas, then plopped back down next to Kendall in his zero gravity chair and sipped a bottle of Diet Mountain Dew. As the song played, Tyler looked at Kendall and winked as he thought, *this is how I feel about you, Kendall, but I don't know how to tell you.*

Kendall smiled and winked back, then reached over and held Tyler's hand. Despite the smile, something about her seemed sad.

"Is there anything wrong, Kendall?" he said.

"No," replied Kendall unconvincingly. "Why do you ask?"

"I've noticed lately that whenever I mention your mom or dad you change the subject.

"No, everything's fine. They've just been arguing a little bit more than normal lately." Kendall got up, walked over and changed the song. She switched to her favorite song from Katy Perry—*Firework*. As she walked back over, she began dancing. "I love this song. It reminds me of the time my grandma and grandpa took me to Disney World. Me and my grandpa danced and sang along with the words. We aren't very good singers or dancers."

"I can tell," Lukas said with a smirk on his face. "Tyler forgot the long campfire forks for roasting marshmallows. Come on, Maxx." Maxx followed as Lukas went to the car.

"I'd like to go there someday," Tyler said. "They have a cool Star Wars exhibit."

When the song had finished, Kendall sat down at the same moment the wood on the fire popped and crackled and sparks and billows of smoke ascended straight up into the air. She took a deep whiff of air through her nose. "I love the smell of a campfire."

"Yeah, me too, as well as being outside in the fresh air," Tyler said looking up at millions of stars in the clear sky. "It's so peaceful."

From over by the trailer, Lukas spoke loudly. "Hey, Tyler, we're almost out of wood. I saw some logs lying around about a hundred yards or so north of here," he said pointing. "I'll be back in a few. I'm taking Maxx."

"Okay," Tyler said.

Kendall gazed up at the stars with him. A few more popping and crackling sounds came from the wood. They sat holding hands while they waited for Maxx and Lukas to come back so they could make S'mores. Without warning, Tyler leaned forward in his chair and slammed the footrest down. "What's that smell?" He sniffed a couple of times and noticed smoke coming from the inside of Kendall's rolled up pant cuff. *A hot piece of wood must have fallen in when the wood was popping*, he thought. Tyler dropped onto one knee and patted her pant cuff with his right hand. Small flames came shooting out of the cuff.

Kendall jumped off her chair and screamed. "Tyler, help me!" She began running around frantically.

Tyler stood up and removed his shirt. As he grabbed the bottom of his shirttail and attempted to pull his shirt over his head, he felt something moving in his right hand. He looked down and took a deep breath. *Oh my God.* He turned away from Kendall and took a few steps forward. In his hand there appeared to be a chrome-colored object in the shape of a hockey puck. While time seemed to stand still, the object proceeded to transform. First it became smooth, then the yin and yang symbols emerged. And then it began to glow an orange color!

Thunderstruck by the appearance of the object, Tyler dropped it. It landed on the ground and emitted a unique but familiar humming sound. Tyler finished removing his shirt, then immediately turned and dropped to douse Kendall's pant cuff, but the flames on her pants along with the campfire were already extinguished. He glanced at the object lying on the ground. He thought he was seeing things, but it appeared that flames and smoke were absorbing into it. *That's impossible.*

With Kendall still crying, Tyler stood

and embraced her. "It's all right, Kendall. The fire is out. Everything is okay now."

Kendall gazed into Tyler's eyes and sniffed. "Thank you. You saved my life."

"I didn't save your life. It's only a small burn," Tyler replied.

She gave him a kiss on the lips, pecked his cheek, then embraced him. Tyler was bewildered, but he kept holding her as he gently rubbed her back. He closed his eyes and a huge grin appeared on his face as he realized that this was their first genuine kiss, and because Nickelback's song *Never Gonna Be Alone* was playing.

They began slow dancing. However, in a split second the expression on his face turned blank and his eyelids sprang open. He slowly looked down at his right hand. The puck-shaped object was there, still glowing orange. Then, in a flash, it faded away. Within a matter of seconds it had liquefied and absorbed into his hand.

Maxx and Lukas were approaching. "Hey, hey, hey, what's going on here, you two lovebirds?" Lukas said. "None of that PDA stuff when I'm around." Tyler looked embarrassed and released Kendall, then bent down, snatched his shirt and put it back on.

"What's going on?" said Lukas. "I heard some screaming and I saw you guys scrambling around." Then he saw Kendall's burnt pant leg. "Oh man, are you okay, Kendall?"

"Yeah, it's just a small burn. I'm fine."

Kendall bent down and began petting Maxx's back. At the same time Maxx seemed to sense that something was wrong with Tyler and began licking his right hand. They sat around the campfire and made S'mores while joking and telling stories. After a while, Kendall stood up, stretched and yawned. "Well, guys, I'm going to bed. It's been a long day." She patted Tyler on the back. "Come on, Maxx." Maxx stood and followed her.

Lukas got up and walked over to his telescope. "Okay, Kendall, we'll be out here for a little while looking at the stars."

* * *

Once Kendall was in the tent and settled in, Tyler and Lukas began whispering. "What did you see earlier today, Lukas?" Tyler said.

"Well, first of all they are definitely hiding the meteorite. They are moving it to

Building 4. I'm sure you'll be able to find it with no problem. Oh, one thing, though. They installed a laser beam field around its perimeter so it will be almost impossible to penetrate without setting off alarms."

Tyler smiled. "Don't be so sure." He walked over and threw another piece of wood on the fire. "What else did you see?"

"There were conversations about relocating Ben. It seems he has been questioned quite a bit over the last year."

"What do you mean by that?"

"I guess he was captured on surveillance cameras wandering around the meteorite at the same time the small piece broke off. But his superiors can't prove that he took it or has it. Also, he was caught slipping a couple objects into what appeared to be an eyeglass case. However, when he was searched and questioned, nothing was found. He denied all their accusations. His security access has been restricted."

"Was there anything else?"

"I started reading more, but the wind must have started to gust causing a sand storm. I couldn't see through it."

"Darn. Well, that's great information. What about a way in?"

"Sorry, Tyler. I didn't get that far."

"That's okay. I'll figure something out." Tyler walked over to the telescope. "How about we really look at a few stars now?"

"Sure," Lukas replied grinning from ear to ear.

After way more time than they'd intended, the boys figured they should turn in for the night. Heading toward the tents they heard a quad runner approaching in the distance.

"Oh I forgot Sean was coming," Lukas said with a half yawn.

"Yea, I was wondering myself when he'd show up."

Tyler and Lukas stood and waited for Sean to arrive. In the meantime Maxx came walking out from the tent then sat next to Tyler, probably wakened by the sound of Sean's quad runner.

Minutes later Sean pulled up and parked. "Sorry for being so late, guys," he said as he removed his helmet. "The battery decided to die on me when I got ready to leave. I had to run to the automotive store to get a new one. I figured you would all be asleep by now."

"We lost track of time star gazing," Lukas replied.

"We were just heading to bed when we

heard you coming so we waited for you," Tyler said, placing his hands on his hips.

"Well, it's pretty late so we should get some shut eye. I brought my sleeping bad, pillow and extra blankets so I'll just crash in the back of the trailer. Maxx can sleep in the tent with Kendall and you two can sleep in the other. Sound good?" Sean instructed.

"Yep," Tyler replied. That was our plan as well.

* * *

An hour or so went by but Tyler was restless and couldn't sleep. He kept having flashbacks of the orange puck-shaped glowing object and the words Lukas had read on the walls at AREA 51.

I need to talk with Pat right away. And what was that thing that formed in my hand?

Chapter 6

Three weeks of probation seemed like three months. However, at the end of it, Tyler had a pleasant meeting with Dean Anderson and Mr. Weaver. Since there had been no incidents and Tyler had been a model student at UNLV and Logan Prep, his probation was lifted. He felt relieved knowing he hadn't jeopardized Kendall's or Lukas's chances to get into the program.

Back at Logan Prep his football coaches and teammates were overjoyed by the news. Half the student body was thrilled. As he walked down the hall between classes, Tyler felt like a rock star. Students were giving him high fives, patting his back and chanting, "Tyler, Tyler."

Now in his classroom, a pre-college course on nanotechnology, Tyler grinned from ear to ear, not because of what had taken place a few minutes ago, but what had happened over the weekend.

Tyler was preoccupied with things other than being able to play football and school work. It wasn't like he needed to pay attention. He was still getting straight A's in all of his classes, partly due to his ability to speed read. But he kept envisioning the chrome and orange glowing object in his hand and thinking of what Lukas had seen. He also kept having flashbacks of his and Kendall's first real hug and kiss. As if he weren't already having trouble concentrating, those thoughts made him want to jump up and down in his seat.

As soon as the bell rang ending the school day, Tyler rushed to karate class so he could discuss the object with Master Tanaka before the other students arrived.

"Hello, Tyler." Master Tanaka greeted Tyler with a smile. "Are you here to prepare for the statewide karate tournament this weekend? Or did you forget?"

"No, Master Tanaka, I remembered. I've been quite busy lately though. But I'm here to ask you why you didn't tell me about that thing."

"What are you referring to?"

"A chrome hockey puck thingy that appeared in my hand last weekend," Tyler replied pointing at his right palm.

"Were there any markings on it?" Master Tanaka asked sounding surprised.

"Yeah, the yin and yang symbols were on it."

Master Tanaka rubbed his head a few times looking bewildered. "Tyler, I wasn't sure the blade—I mean the weapon—would actually work with you only having a minimal amount of Metatron's powers. My apologies. I thought for sure you would have had to have all the powers for it to form. I'll have to check the scriptures. However I don't think they go into that exact detail, plus they are open to interpretation."

"A weapon! The blade!" Tyler exclaimed.

"Okay, Tyler. Calm down," Master Tanaka said, gesturing with his hands like he was doing push-ups standing up. "What would you like to know about it?"

"Everything," Tyler said anxiously as he sat on the floor.

"Very well, I'll start from the beginning." Master Tanaka cleared his throat. "Long ago, Master Dogmai told me about the blade. Legend had it that it had extraordinary powers, but no one had ever seen it. One day, his great-great-great-great-grandfather was working in the fields when his entire village was set on fire by some men from a nearby town. Suddenly the knife appeared in his hand out of nowhere. He was so startled that he dropped it. And then something amazing happened. The fires all went out with a whoosh. His grandfather picked up the knife and put it in his brown leather pouch for safekeeping, but the next time he looked for it, it was gone. And to this day, he's the only person who has ever seen it, until now.

"Wait a minute. I'll be back in a few seconds. I need to go get something that Master Dogmai gave to me and entrusted me with. It might shed some light on things."

When Master Tanaka returned from the back room, he was carrying a very old and tattered black leather-bound book. The gold writing on the front cover was on the verge of being worn off.

"That book looks very old. What is it?" Tyler said.

"Well first, let me tell you that many years ago, when I was around your age, my instructor, Master Dogmai, was showing me how to properly use various martial arts weapons such as the bo staff and escrima sticks. As I was practicing, one day, with my bo staff, I asked him what weapon was the most powerful and diverse." His eyes shone. "I'll show you."

He opened the old tattered book. Tyler sniffed. "I just love the smell of old books."

Master Tanaka continued. "I could barely make out the writing on the cover but it read *Codex of Enoch.* Master Dogmai informed me that there are many fakes, but this book is the original. He opened it to page 423." He blew the dust off the cover, opened the book, turned to page 423, then slid his finger across and down the page and stopped.

"Ah, here it is," he said as he began reading the ancient scriptures. "The most eternal weapon Metatron created was an ethereal and resilient knife which has extraordinary powers. Other angels call it The Mystical Blade of Credence, The Mystical Blade of Hope and The Mystical Blade of Faith however its actual name is simply The Mystical Blade. The—"

"What kind of powers?" Tyler interrupted. Master Tanaka gave Tyler *the look.* "Sorry," Tyler mumbled.

Master Tanaka started reading again. "The weapon can control all earthly elements. And—"

"What did it look like?" Tyler interrupted again.

Master Tanaka gazed at Tyler and paused for a few seconds. "Control your emotions, young Tyler." He slid his finger down the page, then turned it. After sliding his finger across and down the next page, he stopped abruptly. "The shiny chrome-colored weapon's body is round and about the size of an adult human male's hand. Yin and yang symbols are etched on the top and scripture on the bottom." Master Tanaka turned the book around to reveal a picture of The Mystical Blade.

"That's it! That looks exactly like it, except it didn't have the blade things sticking out from it," Tyler said with excitement. "It even had those same markings. I'll have to think of a cooler name to call it other than The Mystical Blade."

Master Tanaka turned the book back around and continued reading. "Protruding from two opposite sides were necks approximately six inches in length with unique writings on them, connecting to a six-inch blade. One blade was shaped like yin, the other like yang."

"But where is it? Where did it go?" Tyler asked.

"It's a part of you. It's inside you, Tyler—well, some of it."

"I don't understand, Master Tanaka."

"When the time comes, it will reveal itself, just like part of it did the other day when you told me about what happened to Kendall's pants catching on fire. It will react to your thoughts, or sometimes it will react *for* you. But one important thing you should know. It cannot be used for killing."

Tyler stared at Master Tanaka for a few seconds and tried to hold back his laughter. When he was unable to hold it any longer, he laughed, then slapped Master Tanaka on the shoulder.

"You're pulling my leg, right? Why would you have a weapon that can't be used for killing? Let me see where it says that." Tyler stood up, pulled the book down and looked at the page Master Tanaka was reading. With a confused look on his face, he said, "I can't read this. It looks like Hebrew."

"Hebrew it is," Master Tanaka replied.

"Tyler, you don't kill your taekwondo opponents, do you? But your hands and feet are weapons when used against them. The Mystical Blade should be used strategically, just as you do with your kicks and punches and strikes."

Then Gabriel spoke out of the blue. "Tyler, you have to have faith in Master Tanaka and myself. As he stated, we have never let you down. Learn from what was revealed to you and you'll find the answers. We can't do it for you. It's something you must learn and do on your own." And then he was gone.

Tyler looked down at the floor and pondered what Gabriel had said. He glanced up at the clock and headed in the direction of the men's locker room.

"Tyler, where are you going? I need to instruct you further on Metatron's weapon. There is more. You need to read this book yourself."

"Sorry, sir, I lost track of time. I have to change my clothes and get ready for class. We can discuss the *Codex of Enoch* later. I think I get the gist of the blade anyway," Tyler replied hastily.

"Tyler, remember one thing," Master

Tanaka said sternly. "All weapons weren't made for killing. For some, the main purpose is defense, aiding their user and something much more powerful."

As he watched Tyler enter the locker room, he mumbled under his breath while shaking his head. "For everyone's sake, Tyler, I hope you read and interpret the scripture correctly. The world needs you."

Chapter 7

A few days later Tyler, Graeson and Kendall, along with many other students from the taekwondo school, were participating in the statewide karate tournament at UNLV. After arriving and checking in, they moseyed over to the end of the gym where most of the contestants were stretching and practicing their forms and fighting techniques. While Tyler and Kendall were performing straddle and front splits, Tyler offered some advice.

"Kendall, when doing your forms concentrate on what you're doing. Block out everything else and focus."

"Okay," Kendall replied as she reached and grabbed her ankle.

"And when fighting, keep your hands up and stand sideways. You're a smaller target when you stand that way."

Kendall glanced at Tyler with her big brown eyes. "Tyler, I'm ready." She looked up. "Hey, you better get going. It looks like the black belt meeting is about to start."

"Oh thanks, Kendall," Tyler said. He jumped up, then gave words of encouragement to his other students as he made his way to join the other black belts.

Bordering on three hours later it was time for the black belt competitions. Because Tyler was ranked highest in every tournament he competed in, he was placed towards the end of the competitors. Throughout the fighting competition Tyler couldn't concentrate, despite the fact that he'd advised Kendall to do just that. His mind wandered so much he was punched in the chest, which caused him to lose his first place ranking. The same happened during the forms competition. His hand and foot placements along with his timing were never in sync, again causing him to come in in second place.

Distracted by thoughts of his grandfather, the object and the buildings at AREA 51, Tyler lost his self-confidence and focus, causing him to come in second place in both forms and fighting. Shortly after the competition concluded, the awards ceremony commenced. Afterwards, nobody from his school could believe it, not even Kendall who was cheering him on after she finished first place in forms and fighting— her personal best. Carrying two second-place trophies, Tyler meandered back to the area on the gym floor where his school was sitting. The students didn't know if they should clap to praise his second-place winnings or stay quiet wondering what had gone wrong. Kendall felt heartbroken for him. Tyler had always taken first place. He never lost.

After the traditional forms and fighting were finished and awards handed out, Master Tanaka pulled Tyler to one side. "Tyler, if you lose your focus and concentration in a controlled karate tournament, how do you expect to deal with life-threatening issues out in the real world?"

"I know, Master," Tyler replied hanging his head. "Even though I lost confidence in myself, I can't let my students lose confidence in my teaching."

"Your students look up to you no matter what place you finish in. And one day the world will be looking up to you."

"What do you mean by that?"

"There are things happening near you and all around the world that haven't been revealed. But when that time comes you must be mindful. Tyler, you need to free your mind and focus on the present. Rise above those negative thoughts. Remember what I told you before. The powers and abilities you have now are only the tip of the iceberg."

"I understand, but I have been distracted by thoughts of my grandfather, the object and the buildings at AREA 51. Something didn't feel right when I was there. I need to go back." Tyler grabbed his duffel bag. He motioned to his mom and Kendall in the bleachers that he wanted to go.

Master Tanaka placed his hand on Tyler's shoulder. "Hey, Tyler, wait a minute. Why don't you stick around for a little bit? In this statewide tournament there will be competitors performing weapon forms exhibitions. I believe they'll be something you'll be interested in."

"No, I don't think so," Tyler replied.

"Come on, young Tyler. I promise you won't be disappointed."

"Well, okay."

Reluctantly, Tyler made his way to the bleachers and sat with Kendall and his mom to watch the weapons demonstrations. The competitors performed various weapon forms from the bo staff and kama to the escrima sticks and nunchakus. Forgetting to be depressed, Tyler concentrated on their every move. He was most interested in the bo staff, how the competitors whipped it around with ease and finesse. After the bo staff portion of the competition was over, Tyler spotted Master Tanaka conversing with other karate masters. Tyler smiled and nodded his head, thanking Master Tanaka for encouraging him. Unbeknownst to Tyler, Graeson was sitting in the bleacher seat behind him, Kendall and his mom. So when Graeson piped up, Tyler nearly jumped out of his seat.

"Hey, Tyler, I'm going to the concession stand. Want something to drink?"

With a *why are you asking me* look on his face, Tyler answered him. "No thanks." But he knew better. Graeson was putting on an eminence front, always trying to portray himself as a nice person.

Tyler glanced over at Kendall. "That popcorn sure does smell good though."

Hearing something vibrate behind him, Tyler glanced over his shoulder while Kendall watched his every move. Graeson had forgotten his cell and it was lying there on the bleacher. He cautiously reached back and picked it up. There was a text message from Payne. *Thanks Graeson for your good work. I'll have a little surprise for Tyler when he arrives at AREA 51.*

Spotting Graeson with a bag of popcorn in one hand and a Pepsi in the other, Tyler quickly put the phone back down. When he looked at Kendall, he could see that she was upset.

"Tyler, I read that. Why do you have to go there anyway? AREA 51 sounds dangerous."

"Kendall, please trust me," he whispered. "There's something I need to do and that's where the path is leading me." He gently grabbed her hand. "I assure you I'll be fine and can take care of myself."

She ogled him with her puppy-dog eyes, then hugged him. "Be careful," she whispered in his ear. "Please don't do anything stupid."

Tyler closed his eyes and hugged her tight. *It's time I stopped messing around. This has gone on for too long. It's time I got what was destined for me.* Tyler sprouted a smile. *I love surprises.*

Chapter 8

A few hours after the tournament, Tyler ate a banana and a granola bar, then quickly took a shower. He rushed out of the house carrying his tattered map and stood at the end of his gravel driveway scanning the mountains in the distance. He was wearing his favorite new clothes—blue jeans, a light gray T-shirt, black and white Nike running shoes and his black Boston Red Sox cap worn backwards.

The orange-colored setting sun illuminated the mountains. He hastily glanced to his left, then to his right to make sure nobody was around. He took off in a flash, unaware that the old worn out road map he'd gotten from his mom on one of their trips to the Grand Canyon had slipped out from between his fingers.

In no time flat he was eighty miles directly north of North Las Vegas. He wasn't exactly sure how he'd gotten there. It must have been either by running or teleportation. He'd been discovering new powers and had started to experiment to see what he could do and had become frustrated when he couldn't do something he thought he should be able to, like flying. However, it didn't matter for now. He was there.

He was standing outside looking in through a half-rusted galvanized chain link fence that surrounded all of AREA 51. There were three rows on the chain link fence. At the top were several layers of swirled barbed wire. Hanging to his left was a sign that read "Danger! Electric Fence! Keep Off! Keep Away!" Tyler bit the inside of his cheek, then placed his hands on his hips. *Great, how am I going to get in since I lost my ability to shrink?* Ever since Tyler had obtained his powers, they had been evolving. When he neglected the ones he didn't need, they were replaced by others that were more relevant. They truly had a mind of their own.

Scratching his head, he looked around. He was stumped, and he didn't like the feeling. "It's getting dark," he murmured. "Maybe I should just come back tomorrow."

A split second after those words rolled off his lips, his eyes began to glow a silver color. Suddenly night turned into day, and he could see everything clearly. Shocked from the drastic change, he stumbled backwards and fell on his backside. *Whoa, this is new, and cool.*

He glanced up to the top of the first row of fence. He had an intuition to jump over it. He stood, brushed the dust off his pants and squatted, bending both his legs, then jumped over not one, but all three rows of fifteen-foot barbed wire fences. He landed on the other side in a sort of a three-point stance. *Awesome!*

He could see the various AREA 51 buildings in the distance. In the blink of an eye, he ran three miles. He passed a dozen heavily armed security guards, who didn't see him because he was too fast, then stopped in front of a group of top secret buildings. Stealthily making his way to the end of the nearest building, he scanned the complex for Building 4, the place where Lukas had told him the powers were located. Spotting it approximately one hundred yards away, he took a step towards it and was instantly transported to a wall next to an entry. He heard the familiar humming sound coming from inside and began to sense that same euphoric feeling he had felt when he was at AREA 51 with Sean. He reached over and tried to turn the doorknob, but as he expected, the door was secured with a keypad locking system. Calling on his computing skills, he decoded the system in nothing flat, then entered the dark, musty-smelling building.

Remembering what the text message on Graeson's cell phone had said, Tyler proceeded with caution. With his ability to see in the dark, he easily made his way through the maze of corridors, being mindful of all the security cameras. He suddenly stopped at a room where he saw something that resembled a meteorite encased in a glass box in the middle of the room. His eyes opened wide. *That's it!*

The meteorite reminded him of Pacman. It was missing a section from the top right side. *Well, not missing. It's inside me.* He could now see the dimly lit room and the glass box that was illuminated from the inside. Lukas was right again. The glass box was surrounded by red laser beams projecting from all directions. On the other side of the room, he saw a shadow appear through the beams, then heard a sinister laugh. *Payne.*

From out of the shadows Payne, who was dressed in a nice dark gray suit, appeared. He was holding a walkie talkie, not a weapon. That seemed odd to Tyler. Slowly they began circling around the red laser beams, always somehow seeming to be directly across from each other.

"You don't look too surprised that I'm here," Payne said in his eerie voice.

"No, not really, Payne," Tyler replied. "What are doing here?"

"Oh, I have my reasons. I figured eventually you would come looking for this." He gestured at the meteorite.

"If your plan is to kill me, sorry to disappoint you, but I assure you that's not happening."

"That's not my plan at all. I'm just hiding from the authorities."

"Once I get out of here, the authorities will be notified and will put you back where a monster like you belongs. In jail!"

"So sorry to inform you, but the authorities have no jurisdiction at AREA 51."

"Well, you can't stay here forever, and once you place one foot off the property they're gonna swoop in and bust you! How did you get in here anyway? The security is so tight you can't even breathe without someone knowing."

"Ha, funny you should ask," Payne said with a snicker. "You're probably unaware that I worked here years ago. I have many allies and connections here at AREA 51." Payne paused for a few seconds, then pointed at the meteorite. "What is your plan for getting past all those laser beams without setting off alarms? I've been here for days trying to figure out a way to get that thing, but I've come to the conclusion that it's impossible."

"How do you know about the meteorite?" Tyler asked.

"Like I said, I have connections." Payne stopped walking. "So what is your plan, boy? You think you can shrink like you did before, then regain your normal size? There are also beams in the ceiling and in the floor. Once you disturb just one of them, alarms go off, and then what? I'll tell you what. There will be legions of armed guards surrounding the building along with every other weapon ready to fire at you." Payne paused and smiled. "You'll be detained just like your grandfather. I don't think you thought your plan through all the way."

Tyler glanced up and down at all the red laser beams, then to his left and right. "Well, my plan is that I'm going to walk right through the beams, take what's mine, then walk right out of here before any guards know what happened."

"Not a bad plan. However there is one small problem with it."

"What's that?"

"You're not too observant. I've been holding the talk button in the whole time. Officials here have heard our entire conversation. As we speak, guards are surrounding the building and once you break a beam, you're done for. You're never leaving here again." Payne turned to walk away, then stopped and turned back around. "This is for putting me in jail," he said as he tossed his walkie talkie into the beams, setting off multiple alarms.

Every door flew open, and like a swarm of bees, squads of guards began surrounding Tyler on three sides with guns pointed at him. He whipped his hood over his head and slapped on his sunglasses to hide his face so they wouldn't connect him with the photo at the guard house. With his back to the wall he looked like a human Christmas tree with all the red laser sights from their guns shining on him.

"Hello, gentlemen. May I help you with something?" Tyler said calmly.

"Hand over your weapon!" one of the squad leaders called out.

Tyler didn't know what they meant. *They must mean my phone.* He smiled as an idea came to him.

"You mean this?" he said. He removed his phone and slid it across the floor until it rested smack dab in the middle of all the guards. As the phone came to a halt, Tyler shouted, "D3 open GE!" Instantly the phone pivoted and spun while opening. A large hologram of Earth projected from the screen and began spinning. Unsure what was going on, the guards swung and aimed their guns at the spinning Earth and began firing. Luckily for them they were using beanbag bullets because they were flying through the hologram and hitting each other. Tyler began laughing hysterically at the guards while they fell to the ground moaning and groaning.

The distraction worked and Tyler started running. A handful of guards caught a glimpse of him and began firing at him. He felt like a target in one of those carnival shooting range games as he heard all the dings and pings hitting against the metal wall. He spotted the nearest exit and used his *Flash* speed. Pausing at the door for a second, he held out his right arm and used his telekinesis to retrieve the D3, then was gone as a burst of wind caused the door to slam behind him.

Tyler had escaped, barely, without the remainder of Metatron's powers.

Seconds later, standing back at the end of his driveway, he bent down and picked up the map he'd dropped earlier that evening. *Payne was stalling the whole time. Next time I'm in and out, no hesitations. I will not fail!*

Chapter 9

The next morning was cool with overcast skies. Tyler was casually dressed in a black short-sleeved shirt and khakis. He enjoyed going to church even if his family didn't go every Sunday. He especially liked it because Kendall was there.

With happy anticipation, he ran up the steps, then through the tall entryway twenty minutes or so before church service. Panning the mostly desolate wooden pews, Tyler spotted Kendall sitting towards the back of the church. As he approached, a beautiful young woman caught his eye. To his surprise it was Kelltie sitting by herself in the back row. She was wearing a long strapless summer floral dress.

Tyler stopped abruptly. "Hi, Kelltie. I didn't know you came to this church."

"Well hello, Tyler. This is my first time here. I've been attending several churches in the area to see which one I like."

"The sermons are somewhat boring, but the people are very nice," he said. "You look very—" Hearing Kendall clearing her throat, he stopped. He glanced at her. She was motioning for him to come. "Gotta go," he said to Kelltie. "Talk with you later."

"Nice seeing you, Tyler," Kelltie replied batting her eyes.

Kendall was crying about something. "Why are you upset, Kendall?" Tyler asked. "Is it because I was talking to Kelltie?"

"I don't want to talk about it," Kendall replied angrily.

"But—" Tyler started, but stopped himself when Kendall gave him *the look*.

After a few minutes, she calmed down and they talked softly about what had happened over the weekend. The church echoed, of course, so they had to be especially quiet. Tyler told Kendall about his cool new abilities and his confrontation with Payne.

"Did you call the police?" Kendall asked.

"No, he has too many friends at AREA 51 so they would just lie for him. The police won't be able to help this time."

"There must be something that can be done," Kendall said.

Just as the organ music began playing, Graeson strolled past them and sat down towards the front next to his grandma. He must have dumped a bottle of Old Spice on himself. Tyler's and Kendall's eyes began watering from the overpowering smell.

Tyler leaned over and whispered to Kendall. "Let's see what Graeson knows. I'll confront him after the service."

The service was only forty-five minutes but seemed like forty-five hours. He watched Kendall go out the downstairs exit at the front of the church, then he weaved his way to the capacious narthex, unable to hold anything back. He needed to talk to Graeson about what his father wanted.

He grabbed Graeson by his arm. "What does your dad want with the meteorite?"

Graeson quickly performed a martial arts move breaking Tyler's grip. "What in the heck are you talking about, Tyler?" he said smirking.

"You know perfectly well, so stop acting all innocent. I know where your dad is hiding. The same place where the meteorite is."

"That meteorite is fair game, Tyler. My father and his fiancé have been researching it for about two years. They traced its whereabouts to AREA 51. They also heard that there was an ancient book which says whoever obtains the meteorite will have some sort of supreme powers."

Tyler was caught off guard. "What? When did your dad get engaged?"

"I dunno. A few months ago, I guess. What's it to you anyway?"

Feeling awkward, Tyler quickly changed back to his previous topic. "Where is the book that they were referencing?"

Graeson cracked a smile. "Do you really think I would tell you?"

Tyler glanced to his right and noticed people shaking their heads and staring at him. He lowered his voice. "You're just trying to make me angry, Graeson, and I don't believe you're telling me the truth. Besides, who'd marry your dad, anyway? She'd have to be a witch."

Graeson smiled and shrugged his shoulders, "Maybe, maybe not. And witches can be really cool."

That Graeson was so frustrating. Every time Tyler insulted him he'd take it as a compliment. How were you supposed to get back at someone like that?

Out of the blue Kelltie said, "Is everything all right, boys?"

"Yeah, we were just talking," Tyler replied trying to sound normal. "I have to get going anyway. Bye, Kelltie."

As Tyler made his way out, he turned back around and glared at Graeson. Graeson half smiled back. Typical.

In a state of confusion, Tyler headed to the local soccer field in a park where Master Tanaka practiced his forms in solitude every Sunday. But before he left, he hooked up with Kendall in the parking lot and asked her to meet him at his house in a few hours and he'd help her practice for her test.

* * *

In the blink of an eye, Tyler was gone and a blast of air blew back Kendall's hair. Within a matter of seconds, he came to a halt at the park. Stopping at the opposite end of the soccer field, he watched Master Tanaka precisely execute every move on both of his forms.

After his second form was completed,

Master Tanaka noticed him standing in the distance and waved him over. Tyler confronted him with concern and asked him about the myth that Graeson had told him about earlier that day.

"I thought I was the only one that could obtain the powers, Master Tanaka."

"Yes, like I have mentioned several times, Metatron's powers along with The Mystical Blade of Credence are the most transcendent powers in the universe. The remaining powers, just like Gabriel and I told you, will complete yours. According to the scriptures you have the marking of the One. Please remember this one crucial fact, Tyler. Any human being can obtain the orb of Metatron, but only the One with the birthmark from God can use its powers. If by chance another human other than you obtains the orb it would place them in grave danger. I believe what Graeson is doing is what you young people call pulling your chain." He nodded towards the field. "Would you like to stay and join me in practicing our forms?"

"Sure, I would love to, sir."

Tyler didn't want to get his dress shirt sweaty so he took it off along with his shoes and socks. During the first form, Master

Tanaka couldn't help noticing several times that Tyler's birthmark was more pronounced and larger. It was about the size of the top of a pop can.

At the conclusion of their first form, Master Tanaka turned to Tyler. "I see that your birthmark has grown in size. Has it felt any different lately?"

Tyler reached behind him with his left hand and walked his fingers down his back, trying to feel it. "Yeah, I don't know if I'm just imagining things, but it almost feels like it's rotating once in a while in circles like the hands on a clock."

"Let me take a closer look," Master Tanaka said. Tyler turned around with his tanned, muscular back facing him. Master Tanaka took a deep breath. "Yes," he said softly. "Tyler, the yin yang symbol is indeed moving in a clockwise pattern. It reminds me of an animated black and white tattoo."

Master Tanaka ever so cautiously reached to place his fingers on the birthmark. When they were not even a hair away, without warning Tyler's force field surrounded his body. A blast of energy projected from the birthmark causing Master Tanaka to fly backwards nearly thirty feet.

Tyler quickly turned around, ran towards Pat and helped him to his feet. As Tyler offered his hand, he glanced up and noticed the same tall figure, this time only wearing a black hood and pants along with black arm bands covering the entire forearms, at the opposite side of the soccer field. Its bare hulk-like upper body and it standing almost eight foot tall reminded Tyler of a professional body builder. And, this time its eyes were definitely glowing red. Tyler rubbed his eyes to make sure they weren't playing tricks on him.

Pat noticed Tyler staring with a bewildered expression, so he turned and glanced behind him, but just as he turned the figure vanished. "What is it, Tyler?" Pat said.

"Oh nothing. I must be seeing things again, like a déjà vu."

"What did you see? What do you mean 'again'?"

"Just a tall figure dressed in black along with a black hood. I saw him at the karate school about three weeks ago."

"You did?" Master Tanaka sounded surprised. "Were its eyes glowing red?" Pat asked.

"Yeah, how did you know?" Tyler said.

Master Tanaka folded his arms. "It was only a matter of time before he became aware." He unfolded his arms. "As for your birthmark, your body is starting to prepare for the remaining powers," he said. "Once you have the remaining powers the birthmark will change again. Then your powers will be complete."

Tyler asked, "What do you mean 'complete'?"

Master Tanaka placed his hands on Tyler's shoulders and looked him straight in the eyes. "Everything you need to know is in the ancient book. It's time you learned a new language." He paused. "Time is running out for you. If your birthmark stops changing and fades away you will no longer be able to obtain the remaining powers. That's why it's imperative you retrieve what is yours—the powers. It's your destiny."

Pat looked down then back at Tyler. He half smiled. "Tyler, a person possessing extraordinary powers—a superhero which people today call it—is what you will become. However, having superhuman abilities involves sacrifices and making hard decisions." His smile faded and he looked troubled. "There's one critical piece I haven't told you. The *Codex of Enoch* states that the powers can only be used by the One, and if they are not obtained by the One for some reason by the time the birthmark fades away, they will be sent back to heaven and Metatron will have failed. Most critical, there will be a short window in time during the transition where the powers could be obtained by someone or something and used for evil." Master Tanaka swallowed. "Tyler, the figure you saw is without a doubt Black Shadow, the devil's most ruthless and powerful warrior, waiting for you to fail. He's thirsting for the chance to get his hands on the powers of Metatron."

"Black Shadow," Tyler muttered. "I never heard of Black Shadow."

"Well young Tyler, you'll come to find out, just as you found out about Metatron, that there are things in the universe you never thought existed."

Chapter 10

When Tyler arrived home, he was still troubled by what Pat had told him, but he perked up hearing Kendall laughing and seeing her eating her Taco Bell lunch with Julia, Jude and Sadie.

Julia called out to Tyler. "Honey, come and get something to eat before it gets cold. I sent you a text."

"Yeah, I got it. I'm coming," Tyler replied loudly. He sat down next to Kendall and ate a couple of soft tacos.

Julia thrust a handful of envelopes at him. "Here, honey, these arrived in the mail yesterday. I forgot to give them to you."

"Thanks, Mom. Who are they from?"

"Maybe it's karate stuff," Sadie blurted out.

Jude chimed in laughing. "No, Sadie,

it's probably from Marvel Comics wanting Tyler be their next new superhero, the teenage mutant dork. Able to eat a soft taco in two bites, the speed to run faster than his little sister, the intelligence to get straight A's in school."

"Whatever, Jude. You're so childish. Why don't you grow up?" Tyler replied glaring at him.

With a displeased look on her face Julia answered Tyler's question. "I shuffled through them and they're from some awesome universities. I put my favorite on top."

"Thanks, Mom," Tyler said, then took the letters into the living room where it was more peaceful. Kendall and Maxx followed him. Kendall sat on the couch next to him while Maxx sat on the floor with one paw resting on top of Tyler's foot.

As Tyler began flipping through the letters he called out to Julia. "Mom, what time does the library close?"

Julia yelled back from the kitchen. "I believe 7 P.M., honey."

"Thanks, Mom."

"Who are they from?" asked Kendall, sifting through the mail.

"Oh, there is one from OSU, MIT,

Cambridge and Harvard. My mom wants me to go to MIT." Tyler was overwhelmed. Even though he was only thirteen he was smart enough and could have enough high school credits to graduate next year.

"Why does your mom want you to go to MIT?"

"She said the smartest kids go there and it's a great technical school. I'd like to go there just because it's in Boston. I've always wanted to go there because the city is full of so much history, and my favorite baseball team plays there. Plus I always wanted to see the Green Monster. I also want to follow the career path of my father, grandfather and even Sean."

Tyler opened the letters. He read them quickly, then placed them and the torn envelopes on the coffee table. He saved the letter from MIT for last. "Wow, MIT is offering me a full scholarship including a room on campus."

"That's great, Tyler," Kendall said indifferently.

Hearing Maxx licking loudly, Tyler glanced down at him and noticed that he was licking the two small scars on his upper back where he had been shot by the Taser gun.

Clenching his fist, Tyler started to have flashbacks of that day. Moments later Kendall patted his leg.

"Tyler, why do you need to go to the library?"

"I need to learn Hebrew." Kendall gave him a funny look. "Let's go. I'll explain on the way. When we get back I promise to help you prepare for your test."

"Sounds like a plan," Kendall replied with a smile.

* * *

As Tyler and Kendall walked to the library hand in hand, Tyler explained in detail why he needed to learn Hebrew. Of course, his friend for life, Maxx, followed right behind. When they got to the library, the librarian, who loved dogs, allowed Maxx to come in with them. Tyler immediately found several books on learning the Hebrew language.

While he was doing his speed reading thing, he kept an eye on Kendall in the magazine section. She selected a *Teen VOGUE* magazine from off the shelf, then sat down in one of the soft, comfortable leather chairs. Tyler noticed three rough-looking boys eyeing her and Tyler while they were reading gaming magazines. Moments later he saw Maxx nudging Kendall with his nose, then heard him making a whining noise. That was what Maxx did when he had to go outside to do his business. Maxx wanted Kendall to follow him. Tyler smiled and winked at Kendall as he watched her follow Maxx.

As soon as Maxx was out the front door, he scrambled to the back of the building. Tyler looked back and noticed the three boys toss down their magazines and go outside. Looking out one of the open windows, he saw one of the guys grab Kendall from behind and begin threatening her. Tyler's first notion was to run out help her, but he had faith that Kendall could hold her own. Still, he kept an eye on her just in case.

"You look like a rich girl so give me your money!" said one of the boys.

"Hello, I don't have any money. Does it look like I'm carrying a purse? I'm warning you, I know karate so if you don't let me go I'm going to kick your butts."

Tyler chuckled. As two of them held her arms in some type of martial arts arm lock, the taller one stood in front of her pointing directly at her face.

"Your boyfriend's not around. Now what are you going to do?" he taunted.

"You boys think I'm just another pretty face. Well, you better think again. I can—"

The taller one cut her off. "Can what?" he snapped back at her as he began to get hungry eyes. "I can see why that guy likes you. You're very pretty," he said reaching to touch her hair.

With impeccable timing, Maxx came creeping around the corner growling loudly while showing his big white full set of teeth. Out of the blue, Maxx's eyes began glowing green, then slowly faded back to his normal brown. He had, after all, lapped quite a few cups of green Dewrilium from that nasty cesspool six months back. The boy threatening Kendall turned towards the noise. Astounded by what he saw, he lost his train of thought and froze.

Having heard enough, Tyler came running outside, then stood behind the guy who was threatening Kendall with his arms folded. The other two guys broke their holds and released her. Tyler nodded at Kendall and tapped the boy on the shoulder. He quickly turned and faced Tyler, who immediately performed a palm strike into his chest, not overpowering, but with just enough force to stun the boy and send him flying a few feet back to land on his behind. He quickly got to his feet and fled the scene.

At the same moment Tyler was dealing with the taller boy, he noticed that Kendall was taking care of herself. With the other two boys still standing on each side of her, she performed two lower back-fists simultaneously, causing both of them to gasp, then buckle over holding their stomachs. While dropping to one knee, she grabbed the boys in the front by their shirt collars and pulled them down and back causing them to flip over into somersaults. As they lay on the ground moaning, Maxx walked between them and began growling in their faces. They both let out a girlish scream, scrambled to their feet and ran off.

Kendall sat on the ground. She sounded winded. Maxx walked over beside her and licked her face a few times.

"Thanks for helping, Maxx. I can always count on you," she said patting his head. She then stood and walked over to Tyler. "Thank you too, Tyler," she said giving him a hug.

"Let's go back inside. I have to put all

my books away," Tyler replied.

Kendall, Maxx and Tyler went back inside. They weaved their way through the bookshelves back over to where Tyler had been sitting. Rounding the corner, Kendall saw a stack of books.

"Wow, Tyler, did you read all of those? There must be ten of them."

"Actually eleven, and yes, I did read all of them. Now I think my brain is fried. I also have a slight headache," Tyler said rubbing the back of his neck.

As they were placing the books back on the shelves and exiting the library, Tyler noticed that Kendall had tears rolling down her face. "What's the matter, Kendall? Why are you crying?"

"I don't know," Kendall replied. "My emotions have been running wild lately. I've had a few things on my mind."

"Well, if it's about what happened with those boys, you should know by now that I will never let anyone or anything harm you. You have to trust me. You have to believe in me."

"I do," she said.

Tyler took out his cell phone to check the time. "We need to head out so I can help you practice like I promised," he said.

As they walked home, Tyler squeezed Kendall's hand. "Do you want to talk about it?"

"About what?" Kendall asked.

"Those couple of things from the library."

"Well, one thing that's bothering me is that when we were eating earlier I noticed that there was a note lying on the kitchen counter that had *Call Kelltie* written on it with her phone number. At the bottom of the note it said *Tyler*."

"Oh geez, Kendall, that was a note I left for Sean. Kelltie called for him early this morning but he was still in bed." Tyler was getting flustered. "Kendall, you should know by now that I love—" Tyler stopped before finishing his sentence, then quickly changed the subject. "Is there anything else?" He wanted to find out what was going on with her parents, but he didn't want to say so.

"No." Kendall released Tyler's hand, then smacked his shoulder. She smiled at him. "Why didn't you help me sooner back at the library?"

"They seemed harmless at first." He grinned. "I came to your rescue."

"Oh whatever, Tyler. You helped after Maxx defended me," she said.

* * *

Tyler and Kendall continued to converse the entire way home. Glancing upward aimlessly every once in a while, Tyler noticed that on about every fifth wooden electric pole another brown and white hawk was perched. This was getting too weird.

An hour or so later, they were in his backyard practicing and flirting with each other. Maxx was running around playing with a tennis ball. As Tyler was correctly positioning Kendall's feet and hands, Sean startled them, breaking their connection.

"Hello, guys. Practicing for your test, Kendall?"

"Yes, sir," said Kendall.

"Hey, Tyler, I received a call. Well, Kelltie received a call this morning. I got the message you left me this afternoon."

Tyler glanced at Kendall, then raised his eyebrows, crossing his arms and giving a quick *um* indicating that he was right about the note that morning. Kendall just smiled back sweetly.

"I have good news! Tomorrow when

you arrive home from school, we're going back to AREA 51. And it's only me and you. I guess now they want to begin negotiation talks."

"That's awesome news, Sean. I'll be ready!" Tyler said. Maxx let out a loud whining noise. Tyler scratched his back. "It's okay, buddy. I can take care of myself."

"Well, I'll let you two get back to work."

"Thanks, Sean. Tomorrow is going to be a day to remember."

* * *

Kendall eyed Sean until he entered the back door of the house. Without delay she walked over and hugged Tyler closely, then whispered in his ear. "I love you just the way you are, Tyler. You don't need any more powers." There were a few moments of silence. "If you love me you won't go."

Tyler pushed her back slightly holding her shoulders. "But Kendall, it's my destiny! It's not something I ever planned on doing. This is the path my life has taken. And if Payne is there, maybe I can capture him and put him back in jail, where that evil menace belongs!" He picked up their gear and walked towards the garage. "I believe you'll pass your test with flying colors, Kendall."

"Thanks, Tyler. I appreciate it," she replied.

He glanced over to her with a smile on his face. "I think I love you too," he muttered under his breath.

Chapter 11

The ride to AREA 51 wasn't smooth to say the least. They were travelling in Steele Corp's dark gray GMC Topkick, and the roads leading to the back gate were stone and dirt along with a pothole every now and then. Sean and Tyler didn't say much to each other. Tyler looked out the windows thinking of different scenarios for sneaking his way in past the laser beams and obtaining the powers. Sean, on the other hand, glanced at Tyler every now and then while drumming the steering wheel to the beat of Keith Urban's song, *Sweet Thing*. After the song was finished, he reached over and turned off the radio.

"Hey, Tyler, I'm not sure how I managed it, persuading the U.S. government to let me and you come back to AREA 51, but nobody else. Throughout my conversations with them, it almost sounded like they were insisting that you come back. They stated that you were allowed back, but this time only. Maybe because they wanted something in return? Maybe they know about your abilities, although I can't imagine how. Oh, they also said that you would have to be escorted by two security guards. Maybe they wanted to ask some questions? I asked them, but they didn't give me a convincing answer. However, the U.S. government is still very much interested in Steele Corp.'s fire retardant chemical and could make me and Steele Corp. a lot of money."

Arriving at the back entrance gate to AREA 51, Sean and Tyler were promptly greeted and signed in, then escorted directly to the large metal building where the fire retardant experiment would take place. Once inside the building, Sean and his two metal cases were taken into the lab where he would set up his equipment. With one security guard on each side of him, Tyler had to wait outside the lab and watch the experiment through the large bulletproof glass windows. He became bored watching Sean fill out paperwork and talk with people before setting up his apparatus. Fortunately that stuff didn't take too long, and minutes later Sean began demonstrating his experiment, which went off without a hitch. The U.S. government and the people at AREA 51 were very impressed and made some kind of deal with Sean. They ended by shaking hands.

While waiting for the verification experiment to finish, Tyler looked to his right and caught a glimpse of an older gentleman swiping a security card and entering a top secret area. He saw something shiny through the door opening that caught his eye, but he wasn't sure what it was.

"Hey, guys," Tyler said to both guards. "I have to go to the bathroom."

"Hold it, kid," one of them replied seeming too mesmerized by the experiment to care about Tyler.

"But I have to go number two," Tyler insisted.

"First door on your right," barked the second guard. "And make it snappy."

Quickly Tyler walked down the hall to see what the shiny thing was. The security cameras rotated, following his every move. Looking back at the guards, he walked past the bathroom, then pushed the second door open just as it was about to close. As he stepped into the enormous room, he couldn't believe his eyes. He just stood there in awe. There were old airplanes suspended from the ceiling. Planes, helicopters, motorcycles, and what Tyler thought were UFOs anchored to the floor with steel cables.

Tyler looked around but didn't see anyone. He began navigating from item to item reading the small LCD screens that described each of the items and the research that had been performed. The first item was a 1962 Corvette. *This car was used for the development of an engine that runs on fresh water and/or salt water. Project cancelled due to threat to global petroleum industry. Experiment placed on hold.*

The second item was a large aircraft. *The Blackbird III, which was one of the fastest jets ever manufactured, was used for an experimental cloaking device. However the cloaking device could never seem to work properly. Experiment failed.*

Then Tyler spotted an old military-style Jeep Wrangler. *The Jeep Wrangler from Toledo, Ohio, was used as an anti-gravity device. Large unique magnets were placed on its underbody which used the earth's magnetic field to make it hover. Experiment is ongoing.*

Then he approached an empty space. *The 1969 Z28/RS Chevrolet Camaro, the pride and joy of GM's CEO, a one-of-a-kind Camaro, was lent to us for purposes of developing a new rust inhibitor. He wanted it to be the first car to become permanently rust free. Two days after the chemical was applied, half the car was rusted along with a few holes. Compensated the owner $50,000. Original price $8,000. Experiment failed.* Tyler began laughing out loud. He caught himself instantly and looked around. Nobody.

* * *

Intrigued with what he thought was a UFO, he walked over and gingerly placed his hand on it. But he was caught totally off guard when someone grabbed him, and the last thing he saw before blacking out was a white cloth covering his nose and mouth. However, whatever the chemical was that knocked him out didn't last long. About a minute later he regained consciousness but still felt a bit groggy.

He was leaning against the Blackbird's front tire with his hands secured with handcuffs behind his back. He easily broke the handcuffs, but he kept his hands behind his back so they wouldn't know he was free. He saw a pair of camouflage pant legs standing in front of him. On the person's right ankle was one of those electronic monitoring bracelets that criminals wear. He slowly looked up and saw an older gentleman pointing a gun at him.

"Sorry, kid. No hard feelings, but it's protocol. Unauthorized personnel need to be detained," the man said in a raspy voice. Tyler immediately became wide-eyed as if he'd seen a ghost. "What's your name, son, and what are you doing here?"

Superpowers notwithstanding, Tyler was scared for his life. "Please don't shoot me, sir."

"Who are you and what are you doing here?" the man asked again, but more aggressively this time.

"My name is Tyler Thompson and I'm here with my stepfather. He's testing one of his experiments."

The elderly man gradually lowered his gun, then awkwardly bent down on one knee. Tyler noticed the name on his badge,

Ben. He also noticed that his eyes were flooding with tears. Tyler wasn't exactly sure he was sitting face to face with his grandfather since the only photos he'd ever seen of him were taken when he was a young man, but seeing the name sparked a hope in his heart that he'd just met his grandfather.

"Tyler, is it really you? I've—"

With guns drawn, two guards burst into the room. "Hold it right there! Don't move one inch!"

Following close behind were General Walker and Sean. Without finishing his sentence the elderly man slowly stood, then handed the gun to one of the guards.

"Nice job, Ben. We'll take it from here," General Walker said patting him on his back. "Those emergency strongboxes sure come in handy."

Tyler got to his feet as he dropped the dismembered handcuffs. General Walker forcefully grabbed Tyler by his arm and escorted him to the door. "Let's get you the hell out of here. You have seen more than enough," General Walker said with animosity in his voice.

As he exited through the door that led to

the hangar, Sean pointed up. "Tyler, didn't you notice the security cameras?"

"Private Robert, escort these two out," General Walker ordered.

As they were escorted out, Tyler glanced over and saw the older gentleman sitting in an office working on some type of gadget. Stopping to take another look, he turned to Sean. "Doesn't that guy look like an older version of my mom?"

Sean looked. "You know, Tyler, he kind of does, if your mom was an old man."

"Come on you two, time to go," the security guard said.

"Tyler, I think you were right about them wanting something," Sean whispered. "When all the commotion erupted, I glanced at their document, and it stated that they should obtain the fire retardant formula at all costs."

"Excuse me, sir, but I have to go to the bathroom again, really bad," Tyler interrupted.

"Over there," barked the general pointing next to the office where Ben was sitting. "And don't make me come in for you this time."

As Tyler turned to head towards the restroom, he snatched the pen out of Sean's shirt pocket and winked at him. Once in the bathroom, he tore off a paper towel from the dispenser, then wrote his cell phone number and a message on it. *Text me so I have your number. I'll give you instructions when the plan is set. Tyler.*

Before leaving the restroom, he wadded the paper towel up into a small, tight ball. Exiting the restroom, he tossed the wad behind him into Ben's office. As Tyler, Sean and the security guards started walking again, Tyler caught a glimpse of Ben bending down and retrieving it.

Before they were cleared to leave AREA 51, Private Robert handed Tyler and Sean each a purple liquid gel pill and a glass of water. "You need to take this," he explained. "It's protocol to take it since the both of you were in a restricted experimental area and could be subject to contamination."

Glancing at each other, Sean and Tyler reluctantly popped the pill into their mouths and took a gulp of water.

"Are you thinking what I'm thinking?" Tyler said to Sean on their way home.

"Yeah, I'm hungry too, Tyler," said Sean. "Let's stop and get a bite to eat. I saw a burger joint that we passed on the way here called Best Cheeseburger Bar in Nevada."

"Well, I am hungry, but no, Sean, about Ben. Get it, Benjamin Steele, my grandfather. He even looked like my mom, only older and with more wrinkles. You said it yourself!"

"Who is Ben?" Sean questioned.

"My grandpa. You know, Mom's dad," Tyler said. "What about what you saw on the document? That they want to steal it?"

Tyler gave him a funny look then asked him what he thought about what he had seen in the hangar.

"What are you talking about, Tyler? After the experiment we left."

"Don't you remembering signing anything?"

Sean shook his head no. "I never signed anything."

Tyler gave him another puzzled look, then thought for a few seconds. He now realized what the purple liquid pill was really for. It erased people's memory for a certain period of time! This wasn't good.

Tyler sat back in his seat, let out a deep breath then closed his eyes. *Well, we left without two things, my powers and Sean's memory.* He smiled. *However, on a positive note, I believe I found my grandpa, and he's still alive. I have to save him by getting him out of there.* Tyler cleared his mind. *That's it, my mind is made up. Tomorrow, one way or another, I will obtain the powers and help my grandpa!*

He reached for his cell phone, then noticed he had a text message from an unknown sender. The message appeared to be encrypted. Using his voice command feature, *D3, decipher*, he decoded the message before even a second had passed. It was from his grandpa so he must have received Tyler's note. With a tear in his eye, he sent a text message to his grandpa. *I'll be there tomorrow. You will finally be free. You will be a prisoner no more.*

Chapter 12

The next day was a break from Tyler's usual routine. He had never missed a day of school, until today. He didn't even care about all the recognition he would receive for having one hundred percent attendance—a trophy, a certificate and his name forever engraved on the plaque hanging on the wall just outside the principal's office. The only two things on his agenda for the day were his grandpa and the powers of Metatron. Since Sean and Julia had already left for work and the school bus had picked up Sadie, Tyler paced in the kitchen waiting for Jude's friend to pick him up for school.

Strolling into the kitchen, Jude grabbed an apple, then glanced at Tyler. "Wow, that's a new look for you. Planning on joining the army?" Tyler was wearing a black T-shirt and camouflage pants. Jude took a bite of the apple and chewed loudly. "You get weirder and weirder every day. Don't you think it's a little warm out for those clothes?" Tyler didn't say a word. He kept pacing. Jude shrugged his shoulders. "Whatever, dude," he said as he walked out the back door taking another bite of his apple.

Tyler spotted the cuckoo clock on the wall. "Eight o'clock. They'll never expect anyone to break in during the day, and furthermore on a weekday." Tyler gave a chuckle, then was gone.

Back at AREA 51 after a two-second *Flash*, he cleared the fences and was standing next to the door at the back of Building 4. He heard a vehicle approaching. There wasn't enough time to enter the security code, so he impulsively bent down, turned his back and pretended he was tying his boot. The vehicle slowed down. The security guard glanced twice at Tyler but kept on going when he saw that he was dressed like one of them.

Once again inside the dark, musty-smelling building, he cautiously crept to the special room. "Okay, first the powers, then to get my grandpa out of here," he said under his breath. He snaked his way around until he was standing face to face with the encased meteorite. He noticed there weren't any laser beams surrounding it this time. "That's strange," he muttered. He looked around and saw a small dusty wooden crate. He walked over, picked it up, then slid it on the floor in the direction of the glass encasement. "Um, nothing happened." He crouched down and scanned the area for AREA 51 personnel. He then glanced up searching for security cameras. He didn't see any. "The coast is clear, I guess."

Advancing slowly, he was finally close enough to remove the glass encasement. Grasping it on both sides he proceeded to lift it up and over the meteorite. Simultaneously, the meteorite transformed right in front of his eyes into a perfectly round orb similar in size and color to a chrome bowling ball. It also began humming and glowing. He placed it on the wooden crate. "I guess I needed this anyway," Tyler laughed.

In no time flat he heard a muffled sound. Lickety-split he spun around just as Dr. Payne and his grandfather walked out from behind one of the large metal cabinets.

Payne was shuffling behind Ben, one of his hands covering Ben's mouth. With his other hand he was pointing a gun at his head. "That glass encasement is too massive for me to lift," he said. "Even with my telekinesis. However, I knew if I was patient you would return."

"How did you know I was here? There aren't any security cameras in this building."

"You still haven't learned, kid. There are hidden cameras all around. They're just not the typical cameras hanging on the wall. Plus once I was notified that a person was by the entry door and the door's lock was tripped, I knew it had to be you."

"Why don't you let Ben go? He has nothing to do with this."

"You mean your grandfather?"

Tyler looked forlorn. He started to take a step towards both men.

"Don't take one more step or I'll make sure your grandfather is dead for sure this time. You're not that fast, Tyler."

Tyler took a step back. He pointed to the meteorite. "What do you need this for anyway?"

"You see Tyler," Payne began explaining serenely, "I need the powers because I'm dying as a result of all the Dewrilium experiments I've been conducting on myself over the past several years. However, I read in an old beat up book where it said that a human having a specific birthmark is the One. I happen to have that birthmark." Payne turned slightly, then uncovering Benjamin's mouth, took his hand and unbuttoned his shirt partway and slid his shirt down past his shoulder.

Tyler gasped in disbelief. "It looks something like the yin yang symbols but not quite," Tyler mumbled. He felt absolutely no pity for the man. "You're a ruthless person, Payne," he snapped back gritting his teeth. "You belong back in jail with all the other lowlifes. Anyway, how did you know about the powers, the birthmark and the book?"

Payne was still pointing the gun at Ben's head. "Funny you should ask," he said and snickered. "Graeson has been informing me for months about you and the powers that were hidden at AREA 51, especially about the powers that have healing abilities."

"And how do you know of the book? There are only a select few who know its whereabouts."

"Why Graeson, of course," Payne replied.

"Graeson doesn't know where it is," Tyler retorted.

"Dear Tyler, just so you know you've been outwitted, Graeson has been wearing a specialized hearing device that magnifies sound. He has been keeping tabs on you without you even knowing. One day, after one of those silly karate classes, Graeson snooped around and spotted your instructor, Tanaka somebody, in his back room and saw him spin the colorful illuminated marble globe sitting at the top corner on his desk. After it stopped spinning he touched the country of China, which then opened the secret drawer revealing the book. The next day after his class Graeson snuck into the back room when Tanaka wasn't there and opened the book to page 423. Graeson heard you and Tanaka talking about that page. He then took pictures of that page and several others with his cell phone and sent them to my friends who translated the writing for me. Some pictures were too blurry to be translated, but that's neither here nor there."

"Maybe the book is a decoy and the real one is with Master Tanaka, locked up in a safe place."

"Ha, ha, ha," Payne said with mock

laughter. "Nice try, Tyler. My connections have informed me that the pages that Graeson took photos of were from an authentic book. You have to understand that I have friends everywhere, even here at AREA 51. My contacts here told me I might be interested in a strange meteorite that glows and hums. I tied the pages from the book, the meteorite and the information that Graeson has been supplying me together, and here we are," Payne said as he raised his arm above his head, then slowly made a circle while still holding the gun. "Oh, and if I may offer you a recommendation for future reference, when you promise people money, better opportunities, or if you have something you have that they want, just like I did, they'll do almost anything to get it."

"I'm not like that!" Tyler said.

"Think about it, Tyler. When did Kendall and Lukas become your friends? Was it when you started to show signs of your abilities?"

Tyler pondered Payne's comment, then looked directly at him. "You're just trying to mess with my head, but it's not working." He glanced over at the orb, then back to his grandfather. He folded his arms and faced his nemesis. "Okay, Payne, I'll make you a deal. If you let—"

But before Tyler could finish his sentence Payne interrupted him. "Vengeance will be mine!" He shoved Ben to the floor and fired a shot at him. Ben rolled a few times, then got up and ran behind a piece of machinery. The bullet barely grazed his shoulder.

"No!" Tyler screamed watching Ben scurry. He was now full of adrenaline ready to fight Payne. However, when he turned his focus back onto Payne, the scientist was chanting words in Hebrew. Then Payne touched the orb with his left hand and it absorbed into his body.

Payne fixed his eyes on Tyler. "It's time you faced the music, Tyler. You're finished!" Payne kept laughing his eerie laugh.

"What?" Tyler couldn't believe his eyes. He stood speechless. *Did that really happen?* He felt completely impotent.

"You see, Tyler, nobody has ever touched the orb with their bare hands for more than a few seconds. Everybody was too paranoid to touch it for any length of time since it was humming and glowing, and every other tool they used to poke and prod it was rejected by the sphere. It gave off a charge or energy surge." Payne stood and mocked Tyler.

Tyler felt sick to his stomach. While he was in distress, Payne suddenly stumbled, then sat in a nearby chair. Seconds later, Tyler heard the sound of many stomping feet. Within seconds, he was encircled by a dozen security guards. Feeling powerless and defeated, he bowed his head thinking that the best thing he could do was to give up.

But then he heard Gabriel's voice come out of thin air. "You must rise above, Tyler." He closed his eyes to compose himself. Flooded with vigor, he gradually raised his head and looked around to assess the situation. For some odd reason, half of the guards had Taser guns and the other half had stun batons. *They must want me alive* Tyler thought.

A split second later one of the guards approached Tyler with his hand out. "You're coming with us, son," he said trying to grab him. However, Tyler had a different plan in mind. With one spry hand sweep and a mighty palm strike to his chest, Tyler caused the security guard to fly backwards, slamming against, then rolling over one of the laboratory tables. This startled another guard, who fired his Taser at Tyler.

Just as the energized prongs were about to penetrate, an iridescent force field surrounded Tyler, causing them to fall like a paper airplane hitting a brick wall.

The hostile encounter had begun.

Panic-stricken, every security guard who had a Taser gun fired at Tyler in unison, resulting in the same outcome. This time the prongs resembled foam bullets shot from Nerf guns, slamming against a steel-sided wall as they came in contact with the force field.

During the fight, Tyler caught a glimpse of his grandfather making his getaway out of one of the exit doors unnoticed. *For the first time in decades he will not be imprisoned. Hopefully he evaded the security guards and was able to sneak aboard a Janet flight.* Tyler had read on the Internet while he was investigating AREA 51 that a *Janet* is the call sign for the flights that shuttle workers back and forth between AREA 51 and Las Vegas airports.

After dodging a punch from the last guard standing, Tyler jumped up and over the guard's head, landing behind him and placing him in a choke hold until he passed out. Then he swiftly scanned the area. All twelve guards were lying on the floor haphazardly. Some were moaning and others were unconscious.

Tyler strolled over and stood next to Payne, who was leaning against a filing cabinet just about to fall. "You have something that belongs to me," he said smugly. Within seconds, Payne stumbled backwards and was leaning against the wall with Tyler's hands around his neck causing him to gasp for air and shake uncontrollably.

With a black eye, a few cuts on his face and a grin, Payne was able to mumble a few words. "Your dog ingested the same Dewrilium as me. He will suffer the same fate." He laughed, then slowly dropped to the floor. Within a matter of seconds he had passed out—or was he dead? Tyler wasn't sure and didn't care.

Cogitating over how he was going to get the orb out of Payne, Tyler heard someone approaching from behind him. With no time to react, he turned to see a gun pointed at him. Whoever was holding it fired a single round straight at his heart. As the bullet struck the force field, Tyler fell backwards and visions and unique symbols flashed through his mind's eye. The last image that flashed into his mind was of Maxx. Now he understood what Payne's last words meant. "Maxx!" shouted Tyler as his eyes rolled back into his head. He fell to the ground unconscious.

Chapter 13

Tyler squinted while he ever so slowly began to open his eyes. They were adjusting to the bright light. "Have I died and gone to heaven?"

Lying on the ground face up, he rolled over into a push-up position and hopped to his feet. He was wearing blue jeans, a fitted light gray T-shirt with the design of The Mystical Blade on the front, and on the back a black and white yin-yang design positioned between his shoulder blades. He also was wearing his Ray-Ban sunglasses and black combat boots. He brushed off the white sand-like substance from his shirt and pants and placed his left hand over his eyes like a visor to block the sun as he looked around. All he could see was the white ground with picturesque mountains in the background. Where was he? "I don't see any angels greeting me," he muttered.

Behind him, he heard a voice. He turned and saw Master Tanaka standing a few feet away. He was wearing a long white tunic and white pants along with a coolie.

"Where are we?" Tyler asked.

"We're standing in the middle of Groom Lake," Master Tanaka replied.

"Well, at least I'm not dead," Tyler said with a smile.

Master Tanaka slapped Tyler on his back. "Go get 'em, kid. Show them what you're capable of. This is what you always wanted, right? To be a superhero?"

"Get who?" Tyler replied still somewhat bewildered.

Without notice, a gold-and-red-colored metal man dropped from the sky, slamming down in front of Tyler. Seconds behind, another masked man dressed in red, white and blue parachuted and dropped next to the metal man. His super high tech parachute automatically retracted into the back of his suit. The masked man offered his hand.

"Nice to meet you, Tyler. I mean Metatron."

The metal man did the same. Taken by

surprise, Tyler rubbed his eyes to make sure he wasn't just seeing things.

"It's an honor meeting both of you," he replied.

"So you want to join our team?" the masked man asked.

"Let's see what you got, kid," the metal man said as he flew straight up about a hundred feet and shot Tyler with his palm laser blaster.

Tyler's force field surrounded him, easily deflecting the blast. The Mystical Blade formed in his right hand. He threw it as hard as he could in the direction of the metal man. The blade spun like a circular saw as it flew, then sliced the front of the metal man's suit. The sparks it emitted must have disabled him because he fell to the earth like a stone. The Mystical Blade flew back to Tyler. It instantly retracted, then absorbed into his hand.

Tyler turned, then ducked as the masked man's shield flew towards him, barely missing his head. Tyler performed a low spinning heel kick, sweeping his attacker off his feet. As he lay on the ground, he placed his right arm out to his side. Immediately, a six-foot chrome bo staff formed in his right hand. He brought it up and spun it like an airplane propeller a few times, then swung it, hitting the shield like a baseball as it was flying back to the masked man. Then he swung it like an ax, stopping the bo staff just about a sixteenth of an inch from the masked man's neck.

The masked man stuck his arm out. "Stop! Nice control and excellent fighting techniques." Tyler helped him to his feet.

The metal man hobbled over to Tyler. "You have skills, kid."

"Yes, he does," the masked man replied. "We would be honored if you joined our team."

"The honor is all mine," Tyler said feeling awesome.

"You must be thirsty." The masked man handed Tyler a can of Diet Mountain Dew. It must have been shaken because when he opened it, it splattered in his face, causing his eyes to squeeze shut.

Shocked from the cold spray, Tyler gasped for air as he took a deep breath. When he opened his eyes, he saw Maxx standing over him licking his face. He was lying in Maxx's doghouse. That was where he used to hide and escape from Jude when he would punch and pick on him.

"How did I get here?" He wiped Maxx's slobber from his face while crawling out from the doghouse, then stood shaking his head when he noticed he was wearing the same black T-shirt and camouflage pants he'd had on the night before. "I must have teleported," he said, still unsure how he'd really gotten there. "Wow, what a crazy dream."

Remembering Payne's last words, Tyler turned and gazed at Maxx. "I'll do everything in my power to never let anything happen to you, buddy. I promise," he said with tears in his eyes. He bent down, then squeezed Maxx giving him a big hug. Maxx responded by licking his ear.

While walking to the house, Tyler noticed that the three huge leafless oak trees had hundreds of the white and brown hawks perched on their branches, sitting in silence and watching his every step as he made his way to the house. Their heads moved in unison. "Again?" Tyler said as he kept glancing up at them. "I think they are conspiring against me for shooting at them when I was going through my rebellious stage. I might have even killed one or two."

Maxx sat in silence and just stared up at them, panting. Tyler stopped and watched him. Maxx cocked his head back and forth a few times. "What's the matter, Maxx? You usually bark your head off at birds." Maxx raised his paw and motioned like he was waving at them.

"Come on, Maxx! Let's get inside before they attack us," Tyler said loudly as he opened the back door gently, trying not to make it creak and wake someone. He entered the kitchen, wiped the tears from his eyes, then spotted his mom drinking coffee. He turned to close the door just as she spun to greet him. Instead of talking, she lost her grip on the ceramic coffee cup and dropped it. She covered her mouth with her hand as an expression of astonishment appeared on her face.

"What's the matter, Mom?" Tyler asked walking over to pick up the jagged pieces of the cup.

"Your...back," she stammered.

"I can explain. I had to do something very important yesterday."

Julia stopped Tyler. "No, no, no. Something on your back is glowing through your shirt."

Tyler threw away the shards of coffee cup, then pulled the back of his shirt up so his mom could look. "You mean this?"

To her bewilderment, the small yin-yang birthmark was about the size of a baseball and glowing. Moreover, it was moving in a fluid clockwise pattern looking like a colorful HD animated movie. It changed from black and white to blue to green to orange to red, then repeated the pattern.

Julia began hyperventilating. With her hand shaking uncontrollably, she reached out as if she were going to touch the birthmark.

Tyler had a suspicion that she would try to touch it, so he quickly pulled his shirt back down.

"Don't touch it, Mom," he snapped, turning away from her. He then hugged her, trying to calm her.

"What's going on, Tyler?" she asked hesitantly.

"Come on, let's go outside and get some fresh air. I'll explain everything to you."

Julia poured herself a fresh cup of coffee, then slowly followed Tyler outside. Her hands were still shaking.

"Here, Mom, let me take that for you." Tyler turned around, taking the cup from her while making his way to the wooden bench swing dangling from one of the oak trees.

When he glanced up at the trees, he couldn't see any hawks. "Where did they all go?"

Sitting on the swing, Tyler handed Julia her cup of coffee. He looked her in the eyes as he cleared his throat. "Mom, I haven't been one hundred percent forthright with you. It's time you knew the truth."

Chapter 14

Maxx came running over and sat in front of Tyler and Julia. Tyler began to explain what was happening.

"Mom, can you keep a secret?"

"Well, it all depends," Julia replied, unsure of what Tyler was going to tell her.

"Come on, Mom. You have to promise not to say anything."

Julia gazed at Tyler as she considered what this might mean. "Okay, Tyler, I trust you," she said at last.

"Like I said, I haven't been totally truthful with you, but remember that time when Sean talked to Gabriel and Gabriel slipped and said he was secretly helping his friend, Benjamin, with a silver metal that he called Metatron?"

"Yes, I vaguely recall something like

that, and I believe you said you never heard of it but it was a cool name."

"Right, and remember Gabriel also told Sean that in due time, something will be revealed? Something the world has been waiting for?"

Julia looked down at the ground for a few seconds while tapping her lips with her finger, then looked at Tyler. "That sounds familiar. But what does that have to do with your back?" she asked as she took a sip of coffee.

"Everything," Tyler replied as he scooted to the edge of the bench swing. He patted his chest with his hand. "I am what the world has been waiting for! The birthmark on my back is the mark from God indicating I'm the One."

Julia coughed up some of her coffee. "What? I don't understand," she said.

"The Metatron thing that Gabriel talked about is real. That is how I obtained my powers about a year ago, not from that green Dewrilium from the cesspool. Actually, the Metatron powers saved me from the green liquid. Gabriel's friend Benjamin, who works at AREA 51, gave me a piece of silver metal that absorbed into me. I didn't want to alarm you because there was nothing to worry about."

Julia sat there mesmerized, listening to Tyler's every word but unsure how to respond.

"The Archangel Metatron, who was considered to be the most supreme of angelic beings, is real. God revealed great secrets to him, like the creation and time and what will happen to the world after its demise. Metatron's powers are eternal. They include super strength, super speed, unique weapons, the ability to erect an impenetrable force field and much more! Metatron had a silver-colored iridescent hue about him, just like my force field."

"Your what?" Julia questioned with a perplexed expression on her face.

"Here, I'll show you!" Tyler hopped off the swing, then jumped up onto the top of the house. "Mom, I'm up here!" Tyler shouted through cupped hands. Julia was now standing eyeing Tyler while using her hand to block the sun. He jumped down and landed softly next to her.

"That's not all." Tyler jogged over to the garage and came back holding a shovel.

"What's that for, Tyler? Don't tell me you're going to dig a hole all the way to

China."

"Mom, please," Tyler replied, not amused by Julia's comment. "No, I want you to swing it at me."

"Are you crazy?" Julia exclaimed. "I'm not going to do that."

"Mom, it's okay. Trust me!"

Julia looked horrified. She hesitated for a long time, but after ten or twenty nods from Tyler, she reluctantly accepted the shovel. "Okay, here we go," she said, almost choking on her words as she positioned the shovel over her shoulder, preparing to swing it like a baseball bat.

"Now, Mom, don't close your eyes. If you do you won't see it."

"All right, Tyler, can we just get this done? I'm not too comfortable swinging a shovel at you."

Tyler turned to his side. "Okay, swing it at my stomach."

Appearing very nervous, Julia swung the shovel as hard as she could at Tyler's stomach. However, having second thoughts she tried stopping the shovel's momentum. Even so, it came close enough to Tyler to activate the iridescent force field surrounding him.

Flabbergasted, Julia lost her grip on the shovel and it flew from her hand, landing on the ground a few feet away. "That's completely amazing."

Tyler pulled up his shirt. "Look, not a scratch on me," he said. Then he noticed a red mark with some blood seeping out where the bullet had penetrated the force field back at AREA 51. He quickly pulled his shirt back down. *Maybe the force field isn't impenetrable*, Tyler thought as an uneasy feeling flooded his body. *If I don't obtain the remainder of the powers maybe I could be killed.*

He glanced at Julia. His feelings quickly changed as he had one last thing to show her. "Mom, one last item. The most powerful ability is The Mystical Blade." He presented Julia with his right palm as the puck-shaped object formed in his hand, softly humming.

Julia inhaled deeply. "It has the yin-yang symbol on it."

" The Mystical Blade has many unique powers, but I need to get the remaining part of the meteorite to complete them, and my powers."

"What do you mean by 'remainder of the powers'?" Julia asked with concern.

"Don't worry about that, Mom. Everything will be okay."

Julia sat back down on the wooden bench trying to wrap her head around everything that had just occurred. Tyler continued telling her about Metatron as the puck shape absorbed back into his palm.

"But most important, all angels obeyed him, as second only to God."

Julia just sat there dumbfounded. "But…but how?"

"Good question. Metatron found out that Earth will go through many catastrophic struggles during the 21st century. Hearing this, he went to God and asked him to take away his powers so he could send them to Earth. Since Metatron couldn't leave heaven, he prayed that The One, a human worthy of his powers, would find them and use them, but only for good. God acknowledged Metatron's wish. God removed his powers and gave them back to Metatron in the shape of a silver sphere. Metatron then hurled the sphere towards Earth."

"So what exactly are you telling me, Tyler?"

"I am telling you I am a superhero.

Metatron. Well almost. Like I said, once I retrieve the remainder of the powers I'll be enabled with all his powers and abilities."

"Why you?" Julia asked in wonderment.

"That question I don't exactly know the answer to right now."

Julia leaned back and pondered, not saying a word for almost ten minutes while drinking her coffee.

Tears began forming in Tyler's eyes. He glanced at his mom. "And you know what? I have all these awesome powers but don't know how to keep Kendall from getting mad at me or stop Jude from being mean to me. And I can't even capture Payne. If I can't conquer these small issues how am I going to handle the dire ones?" Tyler laid his hand on Julia's and sighed. "Mom, there's something else I need to tell you," he said somberly.

Julia looked at him. "Please don't tell me you're going to grow huge angel wings."

Tyler wiped the tears from his eyes. "Funny, Mom, but no—at least I don't think so," he said with a wink. He then cleared his throat. "It's about your dad. Grandpa."

"I suppose you're going to tell me he's an angel and has been talking with you at night."

"Well, not exactly," Tyler replied. "It's much better. He's alive."

Julia cupped her mouth.

"Grandpa is the one who told me about your nickname, Moose, when you were younger. I went to AREA 51 last night to get the remainder of the powers and to help Grandpa get free. I managed to help him, but I was unable to retrieve the remaining powers. Time is of the essence for me. If my birthmark fades away before I obtain the powers, I'll lose them forever. But at least Grandpa is free."

Julia hugged Tyler. She was crying. "I had a gut feeling Dad was still alive. I love you so much, but this this scares the heck out of me."

Tyler patted his mom's back. "Everything will be okay. Once I get the powers, I'll try my hardest to find Grandpa. But at least now you know he's alive."

* * *

All of a sudden Tyler's cell phone alarm sounded. He glanced at the reminder notice, then stood up with excitement. "I almost forgot. I should probably go get washed up.

We're finally going on the amazing helicopter tour."

Julia glanced at Tyler. "Well, honey, Kelltie called about an hour ago and said there was some kind of emergency. Sean needed to go into work and probably won't be home in time to make it."

"But he was supposed to take us on the helicopter tour today! It's been planned for weeks," Tyler said. He shook his head with disgust. "Oh well. I have other urgent priorities I need to take care of, like getting the powers," Tyler said with frustration in his voice.

"It's not Sean's or Kelltie's fault," Julia replied.

Tyler thought for a few seconds. "I'll be back."

"Where are you going, honey?"

"I'll be back shortly, Mom. I want to see if there is something I can do to help Sean and Kelltie speed up whatever emergency came up so maybe we'll still be able to go!"

Then he was off in a flash.

Chapter 15

Tyler was sitting with his arms crossed in front of Sean's desk with a disappointed look on his face.

"I wish you could help, buddy, but sadly, these are very important documents that I have to review and sign," Sean said.

"I understand," Tyler replied sullenly.

Kelltie strutted into Sean's office, wearing what couldn't have been larger than a size two fitted black dress, carrying an armful of manila folders. Tyler uncrossed his arms and perked up. "Here you go, boss," she said as she placed the folders on Sean's desk. She glanced at Tyler. "Oh, hello, Tyler. I didn't know you were coming as well." She turned back to Sean. "I saw the notation on your calendar about a family helicopter tour at the Grand Canyon."

"Yeah, Tyler's father, Trevor, promised to take him on a helicopter tour, but as you know he passed away before he had the chance. I thought since he never had a chance to go, it was about time he went."

Kelltie glanced back to Tyler. "Sorry to hear you had to cancel the tour today. I know you and your family were really looking forward to it."

"It's okay," Tyler replied with a half-smile. She sure was beautiful. "I guess we can try it again sometime. Right, Sean?" he said turning back to his stepfather.

"You got it, Tyler. I'm just grateful to you, Kelltie, for finding these files that I forgot to review and sign. The meeting with the FDA and CDC on Monday could have been disastrous," Sean said.

"You're welcome. And I know how much you wanted to take them on the tour, so I went ahead and purchased tickets for you and your family." She looked at Sean with her piercing sky blue eyes and smiled. "The tickets are for two weeks from today. That's the soonest they were available."

"That's great!" said Sean. "We're going camping next weekend anyway so we've couldn't have gone." Sean looked at Tyler. "What do you think, Tyler? Can you wait another two weeks?"

With a stunned look on his face, Tyler began to say something he probably shouldn't, then quickly composed himself. "No problem, but make sure nothing urgent pops up again."

Sean laughed. "You got it, buddy."

"Where are you guys going camping?" Kelltie asked.

"We're taking a trip to the Sequoia National Park and camping a few miles from there. The kids and Julia have always wanted to see the giant sequoias. Plus, it's a peaceful, safe and secluded area."

"That is a marvelous park. I went there with my family years ago. And yes, the giant sequoias are amazing. You guys should have lots of fun," said Kelltie as she turned and walked away with a grin on her face.

Before she could leave the room, Tyler piped up with one more question. "Hey, Kelltie, did you get a ticket for Kendall? She was supposed to go with us as well."

Kelltie turned back around. "I sure did, Tyler," she said as she winked and exited the room.

Tyler looked at Sean. "Well, I guess it was a good thing that Kelltie caught the issue. And what's a few more weeks if I've been waiting what seems like forever?"

"Thanks for understanding, Tyler," Sean said.

"I always knew Kelltie was a good person," Tyler said with glee in his voice. He leaned backwards in his chair to make sure Kelltie was out of hearing range. His demeanor immediately did a 180. He leaned forward while squeezing the arms of the chair. "Sean, I can't go next weekend," Tyler said with panic in his voice. "I have to get the remainder of the powers. Time is running out for me!"

"Why can't you go today, or tomorrow?" Sean said calmly.

"I can't! Master Tanaka is out of town and I'm in charge this weekend! It has to be next weekend."

"Why?"

"I have it all planned out. Payne is going to be at AREA 51 next weekend, testing an experiment in a certain building. Plus I can't wait any longer."

"Come on, Tyler, everyone needs a little time for relaxation. What do you say, buddy?"

Tyler pondered. "Well, okay, Sean, but I can't stay for the entire weekend. I'll go on

Saturday but I definitely have to leave early Sunday morning."

"Deal," Sean said standing up and patting Tyler on his shoulder.

"Well, I guess I'll head for home."

Sean suddenly remembered something he needed help with. "Hey, Tyler, there is something I can use your help with. The contractors who are remodeling Kelltie's office along with a few others accidentally tipped over a shelf that was filled with file boxes. As you could imagine, the boxes tore open and the files scattered all over the place. I could use your help to organize the files and place them into new boxes. Would you help me with that?"

Tyler paused for a few seconds. "Um sure, I have a few hours to spare."

"Great. I really appreciate it. Kelltie's office is just down the hall. It's the one with all the files on the floor."

While Tyler strolled down the hall, he sent a text message to Lukas and Kendall explaining that the canyon helicopter tour had been postponed. Lukas didn't really care since he wasn't going anyway, but Kendall's reply implied that she was upset since Tyler had mentioned that he was helping Kelltie.

"Oh great," Tyler mumbled. He immediately sent a text back to her. *Kendall, it's not like we are on a date. I'm just helping her clean up a mess. I'll see you in a few hours.* He slipped his cell phone back into its holder.

When he entered the room, he was surprised to find that the mess was worse than he'd expected. "Wow, it looks like a tornado went through here," he said spotting Kelltie sitting on the floor placing files in boxes.

"Yeah, tell me about it, Tyler," she said glancing up and brushing her hair behind her ear. "Thanks for helping. It would have taken me all day and all night to organize these files." A look of recognition crossed her face. "Oh, so you are staying to help me? I thought I was cleaning this up myself."

Unfortunately, since Kelltie was there he couldn't use his powers to speed up the process. "Well, I guess it will take longer than two minutes," Tyler muttered under his breath.

"Since you were kind enough to volunteer, I thought it would only be fair to help. Plus, it's not every day I get to work with a handsome young man."

Tyler blushed as he sat down on the floor next to her, grabbing files, then placing them in alphabetical order.

Chapter 16

Tyler knew the trip couldn't have come any sooner for Sean. His job was hectic and a relaxing camping trip couldn't have been more welcome. Immediately after he had placed and tightened the last safety strap over the tarp that was covering most of their belongings in the trailer, everyone, including Kendall, Lukas and Maxx, piled into Julia's black Chevy Tahoe. As promised, they were going on a camping trip to California's Sequoia National Park.

Getting up at the break of dawn was too much for the kids, so the nearly five-hour trek to the park was fairly quiet. All were sleeping except Sean and Julia. Once they arrived at the campsite that Sean had picked out next to the river, each person, along with Maxx, was up and ready to go. Perhaps it was because everyone had to go to the bathroom. Tyler was the last to exit the vehicle. As he emerged, he glanced upward.

"Wow, these giant sequoia trees are so awesome. They must be at least two hundred feet tall."

"Actually, Tyler, most of them are close to three hundred feet tall and more than thirty feet wide at their base," replied Lukas.

Tyler looked to his left, then to his right. Nobody but Lukas was there. "Hey, Lukas, you said about three hundred feet, right?"

"Yeah, give or take forty or fifty feet," Lukas said. "Why?"

Tyler glanced up. "Watch." Tyler bent his knees, then jumped skyward. He landed at the top of one of the giant sequoia's large branches. "Wow, this view is so awesome," he said while scanning the horizon. Since it was early in the morning he could see the fog lifting all around in the distance. "This is one of the most beautiful sights I've ever seen in my life," he said. He saw hundreds of tents and campers scattered throughout the park. As he kept panning the area, he saw many different types of creatures, such as deer, rabbits, fox, black bears, various birds, squirrels, sheep and even some wolverines.

"Come on, guys, stop gawking," Sean said impatiently. "Help me get these tents assembled, please. We'll have plenty of time later for sightseeing." He looked at Lukas. "Where's Tyler?"

"He had to go pee again so he went behind one of those trees back there." Lukas motioned behind him pointing with his thumb.

Nearly two minutes later Tyler landed back by the trunk of one of the trees.

"So, how was it?" Lukas asked.

"It was so cool," Tyler replied. "It was so peaceful with just me looking over the tops of the trees and the huge mountains in the background. There was even the fog lifting in the distance."

"Um, that's odd," Lukas said. "Shouldn't it have burnt off by now?" He mulled over Tyler's comment for a couple of seconds, then shrugged his shoulders.

* * *

In no time flat the tents were erected, the campfire was started and the smell of hotdogs and baked beans filled the air.

After lunch Sean could finally relax, so

he kicked back in his zero gravity chair as Julia finished putting stuff away. Maxx must have been tired as well because he lay down next to Sean's chair and fell asleep.

With about an hour or so before the nature hike, Tyler, Lukas, Jude, Sadie and Kendall thought they would try their hand at fishing. For luck, Tyler took off his chain and medallion and placed it over Kendall's head, then around her neck. "There. Now you'll catch the biggest fish," Tyler said as Kendall fluffed and shook her hair.

"Thanks, Tyler, but I don't think that will help. I've never been fishing before so I'll just be happy if I catch anything."

"Don't worry. I'll help you," Tyler said.

But despite his help, Kendall didn't catch anything. Neither did anyone else, unfortunately, despite many nibbles.

An hour had passed when Julia called them to go on a hike.

"Oh, here, Tyler," Kendall said as she removed the chain and medallion. "I don't want to forget about this." As she reached to hand the necklace back to Tyler, it slipped through her fingers and into the river.

"Oh, Kendall," Tyler uttered with a sigh.

"I'm sorry. I didn't mean it," Kendall

apologized.

"It's okay. You go ahead. I'll meet up with you guys in a few minutes after I get it out."

It wasn't her fault, but he really wasn't in the mood for this. The one time he had ever taken off the gift that Master Tanaka had given him that was given to him by *his* teacher, Master Dogmai, it ended up at the bottom of an ice cold river.

"Are you sure? I can help you."

"No, I got it. This is Sean's special day. If only one of us is late it won't be as bad. Oh, and take Maxx with you."

"Okay then," Kendall replied and walked away with Maxx following.

* * *

Pondering how to get the medallion out without getting wet, Tyler decided it would be best to get one of the fishing poles. *Well, we didn't catch any fish all day so maybe I'll have some luck and hook my chain.* Within minutes, he had hooked the chain around the pole, but when he went to grab it, it dropped back into the river. "Darn it," he grumbled.

Since the necklace was now much closer

to the bank, Tyler grabbed hold of the closest tree limb, then stretched as he reached in to get it. As he reached out with his right palm facing towards the river, he was astonished to see that the water had begun to undulate with the ripples going away from him. Then, in slow motion, a small reverse tidal wave formed, about six inches high and almost ten feet wide. Tyler was actually provoking the water to flow backwards! He couldn't fathom what was taking place right before his eyes. In a matter of a few seconds, the water had passed over and beyond his chain and medallion. He jumped down into the dry river bed and picked it up. He turned and ran back to the grassy shore. As he glanced behind him, the reverse tidal wave fell and the water gradually went back to its natural state.

He placed the chain and medallion back around his neck and jogged back to the campsite. He grabbed a bottle of Diet Mountain Dew from one of the ice-filled coolers, opened it, then took a few big gulps. Placing the cap back onto the bottle, he glanced around to make sure nobody was watching him. In a flash he caught up with and was walking behind Sadie, who didn't notice him as she traipsed along the dirt path. Following Sean like a row of ducks, the whole group was approaching one of the giant sequoias, which had a tunnel cut out from its base. Of course Sean had to get photos of them standing at the opening of the tunnel. He placed his camera on one of the adjacent wooden poles and set the timer for one minute.

"I guess we should wait for Tyler," he said sounding discouraged.

"I'm right here, Sean," Tyler yelled as he waved his hand.

"Great, you caught up!" Sean said. "Okay, let's start with some serious poses, then we'll end with some silly ones."

Every once in a while, the tree would creak as they stood and posed in and around its tunnel.

They continued to hike for nearly an hour. They were in the heart of the park surrounded by giant sequoia trees when they stopped to rest. Everyone leaned against one of the massive trees.

"Mom, can I have a bottle of water?" Sadie asked.

"Sure, honey," Julia said as she swung her backpack from over her shoulder and removed a bottle of water. As she bent over to zip the backpack, she heard a buzzing, or sort of a whizzing sound, fly past her head, but she didn't think anything of it.

Tyler was leaning against the tree next to Kendall. Taking another swig of his Diet Mountain Dew, he heard something whizz by his chest. Then within a split second, something hit the tree between him and Kendall, sending wood splinters flying. Tyler quickly investigated and came to the conclusion it was a bullet. Seconds later, two more objects hit two surrounding trees.

"Quick, everyone," Tyler hollered. "Get inside the tunnel. Sit and stay close to the sides! Somebody is shooting at us." He scanned the area for shooters. "I'll be right back." In a flash he was out of sight.

A second later he was close to one hundred and twenty yards back from where the shots were coming from. He saw two sharpshooters dressed in camouflage leaning against some trees approximately thirty yards in front of him. He disarmed each of the men by striking them with a plethora of punches, then bonked them on the backs of their heads with the butt of one of their rifles, knocking them unconscious. He checked both men for identification but came up empty. He ran back to the tunnel where his family, Kendall and Lukas were taking cover.

He spoke to all of them as he squatted down.

"Guys, there is a cabin about fifty yards straight down that gravel path. You should be able to make it there within twenty seconds or so. I believe I got both shooters, but I'll go out and take another look."

Jude gave Tyler a weird look. "What do you think you're doing, Tyler? You're a black belt in taekwondo, not a ninja!"

"It's okay, Jude. Tyler knows what he's doing," Julia said.

"If you only knew, Jude," Tyler said under his breath.

Kendall grabbed Tyler's arm. "Please be careful."

Tyler winked at her, then was gone in the blink of an eye.

Stopping about a quarter mile away, he ducked behind one of the giant sequoias. Approaching on his left was another sharpshooter. A transmission blared from the two-way radio he was carrying.

"Red Three, we lost contact with Red One and Two. Stay alert. We have initiated

Operation Hellfire."

"Roger that," Red Three replied.

"What the heck is Operation Hellfire?" Tyler mumbled. Out of the blue he began to hear pounding sounds resembling a stampede. His eyes widened as he saw hundreds of animals and birds heading straight towards him. Desperately seeking a way out of the forest and away from the fire, they scampered past him. He could feel their fur brush against his pant leg. He wasn't sure if he was imagining it, but he thought he could hear hundreds of whispers saying, "Fire! Help us, Tyler."

He jumped up into a nearby tree. Balancing on the top branch he could see why the animals and birds were fleeing. *Lukas was right. It wasn't fog, it was smoke.* He looked in every direction, and the only thing he could see was smoke and various raging fires. He, his family and friends along with hundreds of campers and animals were caught smack dab in the middle of a massive forest fire.

Suddenly a brown and white hawk flew in aggressively and landed on a limb next to Tyler. It spread its large wings, then bowed its head. As the hawk stared into his eyes, he heard the words come out from nowhere. "You are the One. Please help us." With that the hawk descended into the forest. Tyler jumped down, landing safely on the ground as a poof of dirt billowed from under his shoes. "This isn't Vegas anymore," he muttered. "This is a big-time catastrophe. I have to do something!"

Chapter 17

Like a bat out of hell, Tyler ran back to the cabin to warn his loved ones. The cabin's squeaky door made a terrible sound. "It's me," Tyler shouted raising his hands. To his surprise, Lukas, Jude and Sean were holding shotguns.

"Where did you guys get those?" Tyler asked.

"I read the back wall," said Lukas out of the side of his mouth. "There was a secret panel beside the fireplace, probably for emergencies. There were also fire-resistant shields, water bottles, an emergency two-way radio, a first aid kit and some food. At least now we have a chance against the two armed men that have been lurking around outside."

Tyler turned and saw Julia, Sadie and

Kendall huddled under the wooden kitchen table. He walked over and squatted down to their level. "Those two men out there are the least of our worries," he said looking at Sean. "Someone set a forest fire and it's heading our way!"

Tyler didn't want to freak them out by telling them the fire was massive and surrounding them, and he had no idea how they were going to escape.

"I have a plan," Sean said confidently. "Run out the front door to the south side of the cabin and try to draw their attention. Lukas and I will climb out the back window and sneak up behind them."

"What about me?" Jude exclaimed.

"You stay here with the ladies in case our plan fails," Sean replied.

Tyler looked at the women under the table. "We won't fail. I assure you of that."

"What do they want anyway?" Julia cried out.

"Me," Tyler answered. "And I have a sneaking suspicion that Payne is behind it."

Putting their plan into action, Tyler ran out the front door, drawing the two men's attention. They began running in Tyler's direction. Sean and Lukas slid out the back window as instructed. Seconds later, without them knowing it, Maxx jumped out the window and followed Sean and Lukas.

Tyler stopped running and turned around. He watched the men dash behind a tree. Teasing them, Tyler used his *Flash* speed and stopped between them.

"Looking for me?" he said as they pointed their guns directly at him.

"You're coming with us, kid," one of them said with authority.

Tyler folded his arms. "I don't think so."

Sean and Lukas pressed their shotguns into each of their backs.

"Drop 'em," Sean ordered. "Now!"

Both men released their grip from the rifles and they fell to the ground.

"Kick them back to us!" Sean said. "And don't do anything stupid." The rifles were now in Sean's possession.

"And the pistols," Tyler said noticing that they each had another weapon. "Drop them and kick them to me." He watched their every move. "Oh, they're Taser guns." He picked up the weapons. "Well, what do you know? These patterns and markings resemble the Taser guns that are used at AREA 51." He glanced at both men and gritted his teeth. "This is for shooting my dog," he said holding one gun in each hand, then squeezing the triggers, hitting both men in their chests. "This ought to keep you guys quiet for a while."

Glancing past Sean and Lukas, Tyler could see and smell the burning trees. Smoke was rolling their way. "Come on, guys, let's get everyone. It's time to leave this place."

Entering last, Sean took a step inside the cabin doorway when a single shot was fired from inside the smoke cloud.

"I've been shot!" Sean yelled clenching his teeth, then fell to the floor grimacing in pain. Julia got up and bent over him, evaluating the injury.

"That's it!" Tyler exclaimed. "I'm taking care of this once and for all. Stay here and lock the door and windows."

Suddenly Tyler's emotions turned from frustration to helplessness. Emerging from the smoke was Dr. Payne, who had somehow detained Maxx with a choker collar and a leash. But that wasn't the worst of it. He had a handgun pointed directly at Maxx.

Tyler was completely flustered. "How did you get here, Payne? How did you get through that fire? There is no way anyone could have just walked right in and through it. But most importantly, what are you doing with my dog?"

While Tyler was talking, Payne kept jerking at the chain causing Maxx to yelp. Then he began laughing. "You and your stepfather were played for fools. AREA 51 never wanted to purchase anything from Steele Corp. We just wanted to steal, or let's say, copy the formula. That's how I and my colleagues could walk through the fire unharmed—the fire retardant formula, which you can tell works perfectly."

Tyler gritted his teeth. "Stop yanking that leash. You're hurting him!"

"You should start worrying about your family and friends," Payne replied with rancor. "You, everybody and everything within ten miles are surrounded by a mammoth forest fire that will eventually engulf and trap hundreds of people and animals, including you."

Payne had vowed to Tyler that he would go after his family. Now they were surrounded by the fire with no way out. Tyler figured that Payne didn't care about getting out because he knew he was dying anyway. One way or another he wanted revenge.

"Payne, if this whole thing is about killing me or getting revenge and getting my powers just to save yourself, then you can just have them. You told me you're dying, right? You don't look so well, so perhaps you need the powers I have. You would have all the powers, therefore you should be healed."

Payne stood not moving a muscle, just staring into the trees and the smoke.

Tyler was pleading now. "If this is what it comes down to, I don't want these powers. One of the most important things in my life is my dog. Please let Maxx go," he begged, fighting back tears.

Dr. Payne turned his head and gazed intently at Tyler. "Very well. First you give me your powers. Then you can have your mangy dog."

Tyler was about to argue about that comment but thought it would be a moot point.

"Fine," he spat as he willed the small portion of The Mystical Blade to appear.

Unfortunately for Payne, he didn't have a clue that what he was about to receive he wasn't going to keep. He jammed the pistol into its holster as Tyler tossed the puck-shaped portion to him underhand.

He laughed his eerie laugh. "You ignorant fool!" As he caught the puck-shaped object, it immediately began to liquefy and absorb into him. Or so he thought. Little did Payne know that Tyler was standing with his right hand behind his back and The Mystical Blade puck appeared in his palm and quickly absorbed back into him.

"I have everything I came for, including getting my revenge on you and your family," Payne taunted. He tugged on the leash even harder, then removed his gun and slowly pointed it at Maxx.

Tyler held his hand out. "Wait! Stop! Shoot me, Payne. Please let Maxx go! You said you would let him go!"

Payne smirked. "Déjà vu, except instead of Ben it's Maxx. I should have done this same thing to Ben when I had the chance," he said, and pulled the trigger.

Right in front of his eyes Tyler saw his best friend shot, slowly fall, then lie lifeless. Catching a glimpse of the blood seeping from Maxx's head as he lay like a rag doll, Tyler couldn't control his bodily functions and vomited. He quickly spit then wiped his mouth. Furious, he charged at Payne. They fought for almost two minutes, but it was all one-sided. It was about as well-matched as a fight between Lukas and Bruce Lee. At one point Payne grabbed and partially ripped Tyler's shirt.

Spotting flames approaching in every direction, Tyler willed The Mystical Blade puck to appear. He immediately threw it into the cabin, and it suddenly began glowing orange and humming, absorbing all the smoke, heat and flames within a forty-foot radius.

Breathing heavily, Tyler glanced down at Dr. Payne as he sat slouched over against a tree. Tyler's last side kick to Payne's abdomen must have incapacitated him.

Noticing the large rip in the back on Tyler's shirt and remembering what Tyler had told her, Julia hollered out the window. "Tyler, your birthmark's color is fading!"

"Okay, Mom," he yelled back.

Smelling a sewer-like odor, Tyler peered at Payne and noticed that his eyes, nose and mouth were oozing a green liquid. He didn't appear to be breathing. At this point Tyler didn't care if he was or not. He took it for granted that the green Dewrilium, smoke, heat from the fire and the last kick must have been too much for him. However, the final revenge was Payne's. He had killed Maxx.

Tyler walked over and stood by Payne's side. He glanced at Maxx, then looked down at Payne with tears in his eyes. "I believe you have something of mine," he said as he wiped the tears from his face. Suddenly an iridescent sheen appeared around Payne and a large orb emerged straight up out of his chest. The shiny chrome orb about the size of a bowling ball began floating and humming, then stopped about twenty feet away and hovered about five feet off the ground.

As Tyler took a step towards it, Payne somehow mustered enough energy to lunge forward, then reached out and grabbed him, wrapping his hand around Tyler's loose shoestring, causing him to trip and fall.

At the same time, Julia yelled out again. "Honey, your birthmark is almost half black."

Out of the blue, Lukas came running out from the cabin wearing a wet bandana around his mouth. "I got your back, buddy," he said, raising his left leg and forcefully stomping on Payne's hand. "Aaaaaah,"

Payne screamed out in agony. Unable to release the wrapped shoestring from Payne's hand, Lukas pulled out his pocket knife and cut it.

As Lukas's body succumbed to the intense heat, he passed out and fell to the ground. Seeing Lukas and Tyler lying there, Kendall managed to run, then crawl from the cabin carrying the only two fire-resistant shield blankets. She placed one on Lukas and the other on herself and Tyler. She rested her hand on Tyler's back and whispered in his ear. "Tyler, I was wrong. You and the world need those powers. Go get them, quickly." She pulled up the blanket and glanced at his back. "There is only a small amount of birthmark left." As Tyler moved to get up she stopped him. "And Tyler, I do love you," she said as she kissed his forehead. *I'm not going to die today!* he thought.

With a burst of adrenaline, Tyler leaped to his feet. As he began running towards the glowing orb, he could see the figure with the black hooded cloak standing nearly ten feet from it. This time it had red flames coming out of its eye sockets and was laughing maniacally. Hearing rumbling, Tyler looked skyward. All he could see through the smoke and the giant sequoias was an enormous black and orange fire tornado leading up to a colossal swirling black cloud with red lightning shooting from it in all directions. He froze in his tracks. "Oh no," he mumbled under his breath. He'd failed.

"Run, Tyler!" Kendall screamed at the top of her lungs. Tyler ran, then dove at the orb. Just as his hand came in contact with it, his birthmark faded away, as did the orb. Tyler collapsed, fell to the ground and lay there for a few seconds, which seemed like an eternity.

The fire had once again reached the cabin. "Tyler, help us!" his family was calling out. He could hear them screaming but couldn't move.

Kendall got to her knees and crawled to Tyler's side. "I love you very much," she said with tears in her eyes. "You did your best, Tyler. If I have to die here today, there is nobody else I'd rather be with. And Tyler, I wouldn't rewind any moment in the time that we spent together." Kendall began crying louder. "If we make it out of here alive, I promise to always be by your side. We will never be away from each other."

Tyler struggled to speak. "I love you

too, Kendall. I have since the first day I saw you. Where's the orb?"

"It's gone," Kendall replied sorrowfully as she laid her head on Tyler's back.

Then, miraculously, Tyler's force field began changing colors from blue to green to orange to red. It repeated the sequence twice, then faded away.

He opened his eyes and took a deep breath. Kendall raised her head, then moved over as Tyler stood. He felt like he was floating. He actually was, slightly, only millimeters off the ground. He was also feeling euphoric.

Kendall was holding his leg. She almost passed out from the heat and smoke as she slowly glanced up and stared at his back. "The birthmark is back," she mumbled as she lowered her head to the ground.

Looking down at his chest, then his arms, then his legs, he noticed he had become more muscular. He smiled from ear to ear. "I feel so awesome. I feel invincible. I obtained the remaining powers. I am complete. Without a doubt, I am now Metatron."

He heard someone breathing heavily and saw the figure standing only a few feet in front of him. "You have won this time, immortal. Until we meet again," said Black Shadow with a devilish raspy voice. Then it mutated into gray smoke and vanished into the ground as if sucked in by a vacuum cleaner.

Tyler could barely see the cabin through the smoke as it began to be engulfed by the fire. Kendall lay by his feet struggling to breathe, partially covered with the fire blanket. He looked skyward, coughing. "God, please help me."

Without a second to spare, the entire Mystical Blade formed with blades extended in his hand. It was glowing orange. On the blade's necks were the symbols he had seen in his mind's eye weeks prior. It seemed like it was speaking to him, telling him to throw it into the ground, so he did just that. As one of the blades penetrated the dirt, an orange energy source rippled from it just like when a rain drop falls into water. "What was that?" he said as he lost sight of the ripple. "I gotta see this."

He ran around to the opposite side of one of the burnt sequoia trees. He looked up, then jumped and perched on one of the tree's top branches. "That's impossible," he mumbled as he saw the ripple traveling at a high rate of speed. He guessed it went almost twenty miles in every direction, extinguishing any fires in its path while absorbing all the smoke within a matter of seconds.

Moments later The Mystical Blade appeared back in his hand. The blades immediately retracted and the entire object absorbed into his palm. Hearing the squeaky cabin door open below, he quickly jumped down. He looked skyward again, but this time the sky was bright blue with the sun shining down through the burnt trees.

Julia ran out carrying water bottles. "You guys okay?"

"I couldn't be better, Mom. Give the water to Kendall and Lukas." He looked around at all the huge black trees. "I wonder how many lives were taken because of me. I know one for sure," he said as he glanced over at Maxx. "How's Sean?"

"He's doing okay. Jude is with him. We used the two-way radio to call for help. Someone should be here shortly. What about Payne? Is he dead?" Julia asked with hostility in her voice.

"I'm not sure." Tyler walked over to Payne, then slowly squatted by his side and felt for a pulse. There was one, but it was weak. "I thought it was finally over," Tyler said under his breath. "Unfortunately, he's alive."

Hearing sirens approaching, he walked back over to where Julia, Kendall and Lukas were standing. From out of the cabin, Sean, Jude and Sadie joined them. Tyler noticed that everyone was covered with soot, including their faces. They began hugging each other.

"Thanks, Tyler," Julia whispered in his ear.

"Well, guys, this isn't the camping trip I planned, but at least I'm grateful we are alive," Sean said.

"Not everyone," Tyler replied choking up. He walked over to Maxx, crying. "Time to go home, buddy," he said as he picked him up.

"I'm so sorry, Tyler. I didn't know," said Sean.

The driver of the rescue squad jumped out and ran towards them. "It's a miracle, an act of God! All the fires were extinguished just as it approached the line of campers trying to leave. And all the smoke disappeared. I've been working for many years in these mountains but have never seen nothing like what just happened."

"We have a gunshot wound here," Julia said pointing to Sean's leg.

"What about any animals?" Tyler said. "Did any of them make it?"

"Yes, I believe all of the animals did make it out okay, but we're still assessing the fire damage."

"Not all the animals were saved," Tyler replied with tears in his eyes.

Julia walked over to Tyler at the same time that Sean, Jude, Sadie, Kendall and Lukas were being loaded up onto the rescue squads. "Honey, even though Maxx died, you did save the lives of hundreds of people and animals."

"Thanks, Mom, but Maxx didn't have to die."

"I know, but remember, there's a reason for everything," she said rubbing his arm. "Where are you taking Maxx?"

"Home. I'm not just going to leave him here. I'll meet you guys at the hospital in a little bit."

Holding Maxx in front of him, cradled in his arms, Tyler was about to take off when a brown and white hawk rocketed down from the sky and landed on a nearby branch. It spread its large wings and waved them a few times. Again, Tyler heard words come out from nowhere. "Thank you." He nodded at the hawk, then he and Maxx disappeared.

Chapter 18

Rustling around the basement, then in his garage, Tyler found an oversized cooler. "This should work," he said to himself placing it in the middle of the garage floor and opening the lid. He picked up Maxx and placed him in it. "Sorry, buddy, this is the best I can do for now," he said with tears in his eyes as he closed and locked the lid. He said a quick prayer as he carried the cooler over to the chest freezer and placed it inside.

Hearing his phone ringing, he removed it from its case. It was Julia. She told him that due to the vast number of people who needed medical attention and the overcrowding in the local hospitals, they and Dr. Payne were being flown by Life Flight helicopters to Mountain View Hospital just outside of North Las Vegas. Ironically,

Mountain View Hospital was where Julia worked, so she knew much of the staff. She told Tyler that they should arrive at the hospital in about an hour.

"Okay, Mom. I have some reading to do, but I'll meet you guys there. How's Sean doing?"

"He lost some blood, but I believe he'll be fine."

"That's great news. Please tell Kendall I'll talk to her when I get there."

Pressing the end button on his phone, then slipping it into its holder, Tyler arrived at the taekwondo school within the blink of an eye. He immediately went into the back room, opened the secret compartment, removed the *Codex of Enoch* and began reading, from the beginning. Sitting at the desk, he read line by line, a little bit slower than usual so he would comprehend everything. Flipping to page 325, he glanced at his phone. "Holy Toledo, it's already been an hour. I gotta bounce," he mumbled. Dust flew out of the pages as he aggressively slammed the book shut.

By the time he arrived at the hospital, Julia, Jude, Sadie, Kendall and Lukas had already been treated and released. Sean was in stable condition resting in his own private room, and Lukas's parents were there to take him home. Tyler gave Lukas a hug.

"You saved my life, buddy."

"Yeah, but you saved all of ours. That was so awesome. I just love your new powers."

"Shh," Tyler replied. "Not so loud." Lukas smiled. "See you at school next week."

On his way to Sean's room, Tyler caught a glimpse of Dr. Payne through the partially closed door. Tubes and wires emerging from his body were connected to various machines. Filled with curiosity, he stopped in the doorway and peeked through the gap. Payne appeared to be struggling to write something on a piece of paper. Even though Tyler disliked him with a passion, he still felt somewhat sorry for him. After all, Tyler did have a heart. He shook his head and continued on.

Two rooms away, Tyler entered Sean's room. Kendall instantly jumped off the chair she was sitting on, ran over to Tyler and gave him a big hug.

"I missed you," she said.

"I missed you too, Kendall," he replied as he gently used both thumbs to wipe the tears from her cheeks. "I just want to hold you in my arms forever."

Sean loudly cleared his throat. "How are you doing, Tyler?"

"I feel awesome, except my brain is fried from reading, but the question is how do you feel?"

"I'm a little sore but I'll survive." Sean picked up the remote and turned off the television. "Tyler, you did an amazing and brave thing today. You saved many lives and I just want to say that I'm very proud of you."

"Thanks, Sean. That means a lot to me, but I still have a lot to learn."

"I'm positive you'll figure things out," Sean said.

Out of the blue, the hallway intercom blared. "Code blue, Room 323, code blue, Room 323."

"That's Payne's room," Tyler said as he ran to the doorway. Various nurses and doctors were running into Payne's room.

"Oh, Tyler, did you pass Kelltie on your way in? She left a few minutes before you got here. She told me to tell you she's happy you're okay." Kendall gazed at Tyler with an indifferent look on her face.

"No, I didn't," he said uncomfortably. "Um, I wonder what's going on with Payne."

* * *

Two days later Tyler was at the local cemetery standing at a distance just to make sure he was buried and gone once and for all. Yes, Dr. Mason Payne had died from complications brought on by extreme heat and smoke inhalation. Well, that was what the local newspaper printed, anyway.

"I've seen enough," Tyler said. "I have better things to do." He turned, but stopped as he caught a glimpse of someone standing near the casket. "What?" Tyler said not believing his eyes. "That's odd. I don't recall Kelltie being friends with Payne."

He changed his mind and stayed for a little bit longer. As everyone stared at Payne's casket, the minister handed Kelltie a white scroll and a large gold-colored envelope. A few minutes later, after the prayer and after everyone had said their last goodbyes, Kelltie walked to her car and stopped. She opened the sealed envelope and removed a white piece of paper along with a small black box.

As she was reading, she started crying. Tyler glanced back to the burial site, then back to her. "What is going on? Why would the minister be giving Kelltie anything? And what was in that black box? Maybe it's some kind of secret device? Something's definitely not right here," Tyler said. "I have to get a closer look." But as he was making his move, she entered her car and drove away.

* * *

The next morning, Tyler, along with his family, Kendall, Lukas, Master Tanaka and Kelltie had a small ceremony for Maxx. It brought back memories of his father's burial. Tyler removed Maxx, wrapped him in a blanket, placed him along with his favorite pull toy back in a large cooler, which served as a makeshift casket, then buried him in the backyard next to his doghouse. He didn't want to place Maxx in the ground unprotected.

The song *Angel* by Sarah McLaughlin played in Tyler's head throughout the ceremony. This was the same song that had played on the car ride home from the breeder's as Maxx had sat on his lap when he was only eight weeks old. After Tyler filled in the hole and packed the dirt around it, they all folded their hands and stood in a circle around the gravesite in silence. Tyler removed his ball cap, then closed his eyes as tears flowed down his cheeks. Noticing his distress, Kendall gently grabbed his hand and held it. Then Tyler said the Lord's Prayer.

A few minutes had passed when Master Tanaka leaned over and whispered to Tyler. "Did you begin reading the *Codex of Enoch* yet?"

"Yes, sir," Tyler whispered back. "But I'm not finished yet. I've been stopping after reading a chapter or two, then reviewing what I read to make sure I understood."

"Finish it as soon as possible, Tyler. There is much to learn."

"Well, since we're all here, Julia and I would like all of you to join us for a cookout," said Sean, breaking the silence. "We have already bought everything, so we would love for all of you to stay."

"Free food! I'm up for that," Lukas chimed in.

"You're very kind, Sean," Master Tanaka replied.

Everyone else stayed for the cookout as well.

Taking advantage of Tyler's preoccupation with cooking burgers and chicken, Master Tanaka walked over by Kendall and Lukas. "Both of you please keep an eye on Tyler," he said quietly. "He has much on his mind. Call me if anything out of the ordinary happens. I sense the turmoil isn't quite over." Kendall and Lukas both agreed.

Flipping the food on the grill, Tyler kept watching Kelltie talking with Sean. He wanted desperately to question her about the black box but didn't want her to know he was at Payne's funeral. He turned his new World Series Boston Red Sox cap backwards as he took a sip of his Diet Mountain Dew. He glanced at Kelltie again, unable to shake the uneasy feeling he felt. *I have an uncanny sensation that something's not right here.*

Chapter 19

It had been four atypical days since Tyler had buried Maxx. He was feeling out of sorts from the loss of his best friend. His daily routine was all in disarray. He moped around the house not really doing much, not even attending karate classes. He would go outside every couple of hours and speak to Maxx's grave. Each time tears would flood his eyes as he would tell Maxx he was sorry he couldn't have done more to help him. Tyler blamed himself for Maxx's death just as he blamed himself for his father's.

After eating lunch, which wasn't much, Tyler decided to go off and test the theory about The Mystical Blade not being able to kill. The timing couldn't have been more perfect.

Stepping outside, he became furious.

"Bad choice, coyote," he mumbled under his breath. Sure enough, a coyote was standing on top of and digging at Maxx's grave, panting. Tyler whipped his right arm down to his side, then willed The Mystical Blade to appear. It quickly formed in his right hand. He reared back and threw it as hard as he could. Spinning through the air and approaching the coyote, the blades retracted, then the object vanished. A split second later The Mystical Blade was back in his hand.

"I guess Master Tanaka was right." But despite the appearance of the blade, the coyote hadn't budged. "Hey, get out of here!" Tyler yelled.

The coyote looked up, spotted Tyler and ran off. Making sure that didn't happen again, Tyler installed a five-foot chain link fence around Maxx's grave without using any special abilities. Luckily there was some old fencing resting behind the garage. During the construction of the fence Lukas called Tyler a few times on his cell phone, but Tyler didn't feel like talking so he didn't answer.

"There, that should keep any animals out," Tyler muttered as he wiped the sweat from his forehead. He ran inside the house and changed clothes. "Mom, I'm going out for a run. I'll be back in a few hours."

"Okay, honey. Dinner should be ready by then," Julia replied not wanting to ask questions.

Taking off like a bat out of hell, Tyler ran for nearly twenty miles before he stopped abruptly, not because he was out of breath but because of a thought that popped into his mind. He wanted to see if he actually had the ability to teleport. Standing with his hands on his hips, he began mulling over where he would like to go first. Out of all the places on the entire earth he could have possibly wanted to go, he selected the site of the World Trade Center reflecting pools in New York City. A split second after thinking of the place, he was there and began to walk slowly around each pool. He could hear the waterfalls while he read the names of the people who had lost their lives on September 11th, 2001.

Pondering and contemplating about everything that had happened lately, he lost track of time. "If I could transport back in time to 2001, I would have saved all these people's lives," Tyler said as he closed his eyes and saw pictures of the burning towers in his mind's eye. He opened his eyes, walked over to one of the benches and sat in the shade of a tree. "Now that I have these powers and abilities, I'll try my hardest to make sure things like what happened here and Pearl Harbor and other worldly catastrophes will never happen again," he said.

Nearly a minute had passed when Tyler was startled by his cell phone ringing. It was Julia.

"Hey, Mom."

"Dinner is almost ready. Will you be home soon?"

"Um, yep, I'm just down the road," Tyler replied not wanting to tell his mom where he really was and how he got there. A huge grin sprouted from ear to ear. "This is so cool," he said barely controlling his bliss.

He thought of his house, then was standing in his driveway a split second later. He ran into the house, washed up a bit, plugged in his cell phone to charge it, then ran back downstairs to the supper table.

Just as he was taking a bite of mashed potatoes, the house phone rang. "I'll get it," Sadie exclaimed as she jumped off her chair. It's for you, Tyler. It's Kendall."

Tyler walked over and took the receiver.

"Hey, Kendall, what's up?" He could hear Kendall crying. "What's the matter?"

As if things couldn't have gotten any worse for Tyler, Kendall gave him some heartbreaking news. He already had a slight inkling that something had been upsetting her, but he couldn't put his finger on it. He thought she was jealous of Kelltie, but she wasn't. It turned out that her mom and dad had been going through a divorce and she was moving to Kansas. Kendall and her mom would be leaving in two days to stay with her aunt and her cousins Evelyn and Harper. Tyler was devastated.

"Kendall, why didn't you tell me about this earlier?"

"I didn't want you to worry about my problems when you have your own issues to work out," she replied. "I didn't want you to be mad at me because I'm moving away. I know we promised each other that we would never be alone, but this is out of my control. Moving away hurts me just as much as it's hurting you. Also, my mom suggested that we don't see each other because it would just make it harder on us. I'll call you when I get to Kansas. And Tyler, I love you." And without giving him a chance to respond, she ended the call.

The first girl, the only girl he had ever loved other than his mom and Sadie, was moving away. He had a sick feeling in the pit of his stomach.

Back at the dinner table, Tyler was explaining to his family what was going on with Kendall when the phone rang again. Presuming it was her again, he answered it. The phone's LED screen read *Unknown Caller*. Without saying a word, Tyler slowly hung up the phone with a blank expression on his face.

"Who was it?" Julia asked.

"I don't know, Mom," Tyler said softly. "It was a disguised voice. All the person said was that one way or another, he will get his revenge."

Just as Tyler got those words out his mouth, shots were fired and a shower of bullets hit their home, shattering windows. Everyone screamed, panicked, scattered and ducked for cover except Tyler. Fearless, he ran outside and looked around but saw nobody and no vehicles. *They must have been snipers*, he thought.

Once the dust had settled, Sean called the police and his FBI friends. It took the authorities almost thirty minutes to respond.

Sean's FBI friends suggested that he and his family go to a safe house or a family member's to get away from there for a while, until they could figure out who was trying to kill them. They suspected that it had something to do with Payne.

* * *

Two days later the windows were replaced and all the bullet holes were patched. Julia and Sean still hadn't made up their minds about moving out. However, the day had finally come for Tyler and his family to go on the helicopter tour.

Since Kendall had moved away there was an extra ticket. Sean invited Kelltie since he noticed that for some reason she had seemed kind of down for the past week. He thought the tour might cheer her up. Tyler was really keen on the idea but it wasn't his call. She met everyone at the house so they could all ride together.

A few hours later they had finally arrived and were waiting in line for the Grand Canyon helicopter tours. Tyler was beginning to feel exhilarated at the thought of flying in a helicopter. *I wish my dad was here, and Kendall,* he thought.

Standing in line behind Tyler, Kelltie seemed uneasy. "My stomach's feeling a bit queasy," she said. "I'm going to sit down for a while."

"I'll go with you," Tyler replied.

As they were sitting next to each other with their backs leaning against the side of the ticket booth, Kelltie turned to him. "Tyler, again, I'm sorry about Maxx. Too bad there wasn't some kind of miracle that would bring him back."

Suddenly, something snapped and Tyler leapt to his feet. He had figured out what Payne had meant by 'The powers will give him the ability to heal.' He ran over to Julia. "I'll be back," he said as he walked behind the ticket booth.

In an instant, Tyler had arrived back home. Apparently, Lukas had climbed over the fence, since he was kneeling by Maxx's grave smoothing out the dirt. When he saw Tyler, he was so startled that he almost fell over.

"What are you doing here? I thought you were going on the helicopter tour," he said.

Tyler was frantic. "Follow me. We need some shovels." Then, unbeknownst to Tyler, his cell phone fell off his belt. The boys returned to the gravesite and unearthed Maxx. Tyler pulled out the big plastic cooler he had buried Maxx in. They sat there for a few seconds, then removed the lid.

"Holy Toledo," Lukas muttered as he began gagging. The smell of the decaying carcass seeped from the plastic cooler and penetrated their noses. Tyler also cringed and squirmed and began gagging. They boys both plugged their noses. Tyler removed Maxx's favorite rubber pull toy, then picked up Maxx, who was wrapped in his favorite black fuzzy blanket, and placed him on the ground. Lukas looked back and forth from Tyler to Maxx. "What's next?" he said with a perplexed look on his face.

"I'm not sure, Lukas. I guess I should have read the entire book," Tyler said somberly.

"What book?" Lukas asked.

"Oh, I'll tell you later."

Then out of nowhere, Tyler heard Gabriel's voice. "Tyler, speak from your heart."

Tyler looked around for more information, but Gabriel was gone. "Okay, here we go," he said and began to remove the blanket Maxx was wrapped in. He slowly placed his right hand on Maxx's side.

"I wanted to say I love you, Maxx. You were my best friend." A few tears were trickling down his cheeks. He wiped them with the back of his hand, then reached back down while closing his eyes. "Lord, I wish there was something I could do."

At the exact moment he opened his eyes, Tyler saw a bright, almost blinding, iridescent sheen appear around his hand, the same hand resting on Maxx's side, but only for a few seconds. It quickly faded away. Immediately, the boys jumped to their feet, impatiently waiting for something to happen. Fifteen seconds went by, then thirty, but still nothing happened.

Tyler looked at Lukas. "I don't understand. Why didn't it work?"

"At least you gave it your best shot," Lukas said as he hugged Tyler.

"Maybe—" Tyler began to say, when both he and Lukas heard some whining. They turned and saw Maxx moving.

Moments later, Maxx's bullet wound healed and the bullet popped out from his body. His natural color returned and he began twitching and wiggling. Suddenly he stood up, barked once, then balanced on his hind legs licking Tyler's face. Tyler and

Lukas, well mostly Tyler, were choked up.

"This is so awesome! Maxx is alive! Thank you!" Tyler shouted, then dropped to his knees and hugged Maxx. "This is one of the best days of my life!"

Chapter 20

Julia tried calling Tyler on his cell several times but couldn't get hold of him. Tyler heard his phone ringing with his mom's unique ring tone, but he was having too much fun celebrating, rolling around with Maxx and acting like a kid on Christmas morning, so he ignored it. He glanced over at Lukas.

"You need any help?"

"Nope, I got it, buddy," Lukas said putting the shovels back into the garage.

Tyler was rubbing Maxx's belly when he noticed that on his way back out, Lukas was glancing over at Kelltie's SUV and mumbling something.

"What are you mumbling about, Lukas?" he said loudly.

"There's some fresh writing on the front

driver's side door." Lukas walked over to get a closer look and began reading to himself, but stopped abruptly. "Tyler, you better come over here."

Tyler got up off the ground and ran over with Maxx following closely.

"What does it say?"

"It says, *Tyler might have powers and can't be killed but his family doesn't. If you're reading this I wasn't successful or didn't make it. Kill them, kill them all. I want my revenge. My intentions were sincere so keep the engagement ring to remember me by. My new formula is locked in our secret location. Stealing those FR23 cases was brilliant! All my love, Mason.*"

Lukas took a deep breath. "Tyler, we have a huge problem!"

Tyler heard his phone chirping. "Open," he commanded and the cell phone projected a text message from his mom. He ran over, picked up his phone from off the ground and began reading.

Kelltie is sick and won't be going. You won't be either if you don't hurry!

"Oh no," Tyler exclaimed with a blank look on his face. Putting two and two together, he dropped the phone. "She's going to sabotage the helicopter! Kelltie was

Payne's fiancé! What an idiot I've been, Lukas. I can't believe I didn't see any signs. If anything happens to them I won't be able to forgive myself." Tyler felt sick to his stomach remembering the day his father was killed.

At the same time, back at the Grand Canyon the helicopter took off without Tyler because they couldn't wait any longer. The tour company had to stay on schedule. Tyler quickly teleported back behind the ticket booth but was too late. The helicopter was already hovering over the canyon. He ran, then jumped up and stood on the guard rail waving his arms frantically while hollering, "Stop, stop!"

He watched as the helicopter banked around, then flew out of sight. He ran around the area wildly trying to locate Kelltie. Finally he ran over to the ticket booth.

"Excuse me, sir. Have you seen a woman around here that was sick and couldn't go on the tour?"

"Yes, she left a few minutes ago. And she dropped these," the man replied holding a screw driver and utility knife in his hand.

While Tyler was standing there, a

distress call from the two-way radio on one of the helicopters came over the speaker in the ticket booth. "Base, we lost throttle control and we're going down!" Seconds later a huge explosion was heard and Tyler could see a billowing plume of smoke and fire from down in the canyon. People ducked as they plugged their ears. Tyler hopped the guardrail and ran over to the edge of the canyon. He could see the burning helicopter. He willed, then threw The Mystical Blade towards it. The billow of smoke disappeared.

Just as he was about to teleport to the crash site, he was restrained by several police officers who just happened to be there eating. He wanted to use his powers but it was too risky. A split second later the blade was back in his hand, then quickly retracted and absorbed into his palm.

He heard one of the rangers comment. "Since the helicopter had just refueled, their bodies were probably burned beyond recognition."

There were numerous park rangers and fire vehicles entering the parking lot. Tyler scanned the area for Kelltie but she wasn't there. *She is probably long gone by now*, he thought to himself.

Standing helplessly in front of the barricade with the other bystanders, he was given the tragic news. A little over an hour after the crash, the rescue crew had emerged from the canyon empty-handed. Helicopter number 3366, which was carrying his family, had crashed, and everyone inside, including the pilot, was dead. Tyler screamed hysterically upon hearing the news of his family's demise. Dropping to his knees, he sobbed uncontrollably.

Tyler muttered, "I love you guys. I can't live without you." He placed his face in his hands and continued with a quivering cry. "I couldn't even save you guys if I'd gotten to you in time. According to the *Codex of Enoch,* being the One has another meaning. I can only resurrect one life a year. I guess there are limits to my powers"

Tyler could hear several police officers and firefighters crying and sniffing as well. There wasn't a dry eye at the scene.

As Tyler cried he felt a hand from behind softly squeeze his shoulder. It was Master Tanaka.

"How did you know?" Tyler asked.

"Lukas called me from your cell phone and told me what he read."

Tyler was confused. Where would he go? What would he do?

"Tyler, you must know. The *Codex of Enoch* holds the key to all your questions."

Tyler stood up and hugged Master Tanaka. "It's not fair! I have these powers and I can't even save the people I love."

Master Tanaka put his hands on Tyler's shoulders and gently pushed him back. "Tyler, we never said this would be fair or easy. And I know you don't want to hear this, but even with your amazing powers you still can't save everyone. You have the powers of Metatron and you can do many incredible things—things you never dreamed of. Use your powers wisely and use them as often as possible. Like I stated before, people around the world need your help. You need to read the entire book. Rise above."

Master Tanaka paused for a few seconds, then looked Tyler in his eyes. "Tyler, you have now been bequeathed all of Metatron's powers. You are a superhero or whatever you want to call yourself. But for certain you are the One. You are Metatron. Gabriel and I are very proud of you. I'm sure your family and Kendall are very proud of you as well."

"But what if I'm not ready to reveal myself to the world?"

"You will read in the book that an epic event will occur. Something the world has never seen before. There will be no choice."

"What will happen?" Tyler said.

"Be patient, Tyler. There is time."

Anger blazed in Tyler's eyes. "Kelltie will pay for what she's done. She killed my entire family!"

Master Tanaka handed Tyler a piece of paper. "You need to vacate this area for a while," he said calmly. "You and Maxx must go to the address that's written on this paper. It's a friend's house in Montrose, New York. My friend will be expecting you. Take as much time as you need to settle down and compose yourself. I'll contact you in a few weeks." He looked Tyler in the eyes. "Metatron, rise above. You are now the most powerful being in the universe, second only to God. We'll figure things out together. I know what you're thinking, but I know you'll make the right decision. When we meet again, the training of your life will begin."

Tyler closed his eyes. Then in an instant he disappeared. Reappearing in his bedroom, he collected some of his stuff, then placed it in his karate duffel bag. He couldn't take too much since he could only teleport with whatever he was holding. Once finished, he ran downstairs, out the back door, then outside where Maxx was sitting waiting for him. He glanced down at the note, then swung the duffel bag over his shoulder. He bent down and picked up Maxx, cradling him in both arms. He glanced at the note, and in an instant, disappeared.

* * *

Moments later Tyler and Maxx were standing side by side looking through a huge black iron gate. On the other side was a long concrete driveway lined with beautiful maple trees that led to a white towering awesome looking Japanese castle. The castle reminded Tyler of the photograph of the Himeji Castle his mom and dad had visited on their honeymoon. To the left of the castle there was an enormous seven-car garage. Out of the corner of his eye, Tyler saw an old beat up, rusted Camaro coming down the driveway. The gates began opening, half sliding to each side. Stopping about ten feet from the gate, the car backfired.

"What a piece of junk," Tyler said to Maxx.

Two people slowly exited the car, one from each side. The driver removed his sunglasses.

"Welcome, Tyler and Maxx. We've been expecting you."

Simultaneously Tyler's jaw and his duffel bag dropped and he began crying. Maxx ran over and sat next to the younger gentleman. Tyler ran to the driver and hugged him.

"Grandpa! You're alive!" Seconds later Tyler pulled back. "How is your shoulder?"

"It's fine, Tyler."

"And who is this?" Tyler glanced over to the other gentleman.

"Tyler, this is Master Dogmai," Benjamin replied.

Master Dogmai reached out his hand. "I very pleased to meet you, my son." Tyler and Master Dogmai shook hands.

"But you're Master Tanaka's instructor. You look like you're twenty-five. I figured you died long ago."

Master Dogmai smiled. "Tyler, I thought by now you would have figured it out.

However, I wanted to meet you and tell you to always rise above and keep the faith. But most important, do not be enticed by evil." With that Master Dogmai vanished into thin air right before his eyes.

"Tyler, there's much you need to learn," Benjamin said. "Master Tanaka will be here in a few days."

At the exact same moment, hundreds of brown and white hawks plummeted from the sky, screeching. Tyler immediately took a defensive stance, protecting his body with his arms. "Don't worry, Tyler. They have forgiven you years ago for shooting at them." Then, as they were about to land on the ground, they transformed into people.

Master Dogmai reappeared and was standing beside Tyler. "One last thing. I, along with your angel friends, have been waiting for you, Metatron." He glanced at all the people standing in front of them. "We all feel something evil is lurking just over the horizon. However, with you here now, we'll endure." Master Dogmai once again vanished into thin air.

* * *

Funny, it was obvious now. All of it.

How could he ever have doubted himself? He would have to relinquish his feelings of enmity towards Kelltie, of course. In spite of losing his family, he had to rise above. But knowing that he now had the ability to take action against worldwide, life-threatening perils, he felt his soul lift. The only question was not if but when they would arise…

* * *

Walking towards the old beat-up rusted Camaro Tyler had a puzzled look on his face as he glanced over to Benjamin. "Hey grandpa, I have a crazy question for you. Was that a real UFO I saw in that big room where you handcuffed me at AREA 51?"

Benjamin smiled. "Yes it was, Tyler. If you think that is crazy, what I tell you next will really rock your world…"

~ * ~

If you enjoyed this book, please consider writing a short review and posting it on your favorite review site(s). Reviews are very helpful to other readers and are greatly appreciated by authors, especially me. When you post a review, drop me an email and let me know and I may feature part of it on my blog/site. Thank you.

laurence.stjohn@yahoo.com

Message from the Author

Dear Reader,

I sincerely appreciate you taking the time to read my novel. I hope you loved reading *Metatron: The Mystical Blade* as much as I loved writing it.

Some of the characters in this story were loosely based on and inspired by real people. I think Tyler's character echoes the thoughts of many kids his age in the real world trying to find their place to fit in. And like Tyler, remember whatever you do, you can rise above your doubts and attain anything you set your mind on doing.

I hope after you read this book it has made some kind of positive impact on your life, just as much as it's had on mine by writing it.

Again, thank you for going along for the ride with Tyler and friends; however, the ride isn't over…stay tuned!

Sincerely,

Laurence St. John

About the Author

Laurence St. John is a graduate of Owens State Community College and currently works as an Administrations Manager, though he is turning his efforts fully to writing.

In 2006, the same year his first granddaughter was born, which he described as one of the most uplifting moments of his life, Laurence became determined to write his stories on paper.

Three and a half years later he had written his first manuscript, *Metatron: The Angel Has Risen*, which is a bestseller. He has followed this with book two in the Metatron series, *Metatron: The Mystical Blade*. He is currently writing book three in the Metatron series.

Laurence currently lives in Northwood, Ohio, with his wife, Julie. His son, Joe, is married to Cari and they have three daughters, Kendall, Sadie and Harper. His daughter, Janelle, is married to Andrew and they have one son, Elijah, and a daughter, Evelyn.

Website: http://www.laurencestjohn.com
Blog: http://laurencestjohn.blogspot.com
Twitter: http://twitter.com/laurencestjohn

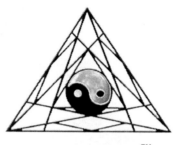

IMAJIN BOOKS™
Quality fiction beyond your wildest dreams

For your next eBook or paperback purchase, please visit:

www.imajinbooks.com

www.imajinbooks.blogspot.com

www.twitter.com/imajinbooks

www.facebook.com/imajinbooks

Ogopogo Books™, an imprint of Imajin Books®

www.OgopogoBooks.com

CPSIA information can be obtained
at www.ICGtesting.com
Printed in the USA
FFOW03n2107271117
43810342-42728FF